T3-BHD-686

"So it's marriage you want, is it?"

Jay's lips curled in a dangerous smile. "Well, then, it's marriage you shall have. The only way to make sure this ranch is safe, to stop you from squandering its wealth, is to marry you myself!"

Natasha stared at him, her eyes darkening with shock. "Marry you? No...I can't! You can't make me. You don't love me."

"Love?" His eyes widened in disbelief. "You dare to say that to me? You, who have given your body to who knows how many men for greed and possibly worse?"

"You can't marry me, Jay," Natasha protested again, hating the way her stomach muscles quivered and knotted inside her. Not for all the wrong reasons, she thought miserably.

"I can," Jay contradicted her flatly. "And I will."

PENNY JORDAN was constantly in trouble in school because of her inability to stop daydreaming—especially during French lessons. In her teens she was an avid romance reader, although it didn't occur to her to try writing one herself until she was older. "My first half-dozen attempts ended up ingloriously," she remembers, "but I persevered, and one manuscript was finished." She plucked up the courage to send it to a publisher, convinced her book would be rejected. It wasn't, and the rest is history! Penny is married and lives in Cheshire.

Books by Penny Jordan

Don't miss any of our special offers. Write to us at the following address for information on our newest releases.

Harlequin Reader Service
901 Fuhrmann Blvd., P.O. Box 1397, Buffalo, NY 14240
Canadian address: P.O. Box 603,
Fort Erie, Ont. L2A 5X3

PENNY JORDAN

fight for love

Harlequin Books

TORONTO • NEW YORK • LONDON
AMSTERDAM • PARIS • SYDNEY • HAMBURG
STOCKHOLM • ATHENS • TOKYO • MILAN

Harlequin Presents first edition July 1988
ISBN 0-373-11089-8

Original hardcover edition published in 1987
by Mills & Boon Limited

Copyright © 1987 by Penny Jordan. All rights reserved.
Except for use in any review, the reproduction or utilization
of this work in whole or in part in any form by any electronic,
mechanical or other means, now known or hereafter invented,
including xerography, photocopying and recording,
or in any information storage or retrieval system, is forbidden without
the permission of the publisher, Harlequin Enterprises Limited,
225 Duncan Mill Road, Don Mills, Ontario, Canada M3B 3K9.

All the characters in this book have no existence outside the
imagination of the author and have no relation whatsoever to
anyone bearing the same name or names. They are not even
distantly inspired by any individual known or unknown to the
author, and all incidents are pure invention.

® are Trademarks registered in the United States Patent and
Trademark Office and in other countries.

Printed in U.S.A.

of boss and employee were she to indicate to him that she wished him to do so.

She also knew that most of her friends would consider him a good catch—excellent husband material. He was independently comfortably off. He owned a pleasant house in a Chelsea mews, and it was being rumoured that within the next five years, he would be invited on to the board of the gallery which he now managed. So why did she continue to hold him at arm's length? He was the right age for her, and good-looking in a blond, languid fashion, but if she was ever to tell him of this deep need inside her to live on the land, to be part of it and its cycle, she knew that he just wouldn't understand.

Perhaps her looks were to blame for that. She just didn't look the way men visualised a farmer's daughter *should* look.

She was just over average height and willow-slim, her cloud of dark red hair curling lavishly on to her shoulders when it wasn't constrained into the chic chignon she wore for work. Her eyes were long and slightly slanting, a deep tawny-gold, like those of a jungle cat. Her face had the sort of bone structure loved by the modelling world. As a teenager it had been suggested, in fact, that she *should* model, but she hadn't been interested. She had been in love then. She smiled a little wryly for her teenage self. The object of her affections had been the son of another local farmer, but Rob, a sturdy Cheshire lad with his head set firmly on his shoulders, had not been interested in her. However, by the time her teenage crush on him had faded, her parents were dead, and she was living away from

Cheshire in the care of the aunt and uncle who had taken her into their London home.

They had retired now to Spain, and to all intents and purposes she was on her own.

So why didn't she give Adam the encouragement he was waiting for? He would make a good husband and father, and she wanted children . . . a family . . . Maybe it was because he didn't represent enough challenge . . . She smiled wryly to herself and turned to study her letter again.

Fortunately, this morning she was not due into the gallery until mid-morning, since they never did much business so early in the week.

The letter *must* be from Tip Travers, although why on earth the old Texan should be writing to her . . .

At his behest she had acted as his guide while he was in London, showing him most of the more famous sights. Once she got used to his abrasive manner she had enjoyed his company, although always firmly refusing the money he offered her in exchange for her time.

By the end of his week's stay, a mutual respect had built up between them. She had told him about her parents' death, and about her longing to return to the land, and he had told her about the massive ranch he owned near the Rio Grande; about the oil that had been found on it, and about the feud that had broken out between his sons because of it.

One of them had become president of the oil company and one of them had remained on the ranch, and as she listened to him, Natasha had known that, like her, Tip's first love had been the land and his cattle.

Now both his sons were dead, and the oil company had passed into other hands. His grandson ran the ranch and, although nothing had been said, Natasha had noticed the way the old man's face tightened with pain when he mentioned his family and she guessed that there were still many unresolved conflicts within it.

She had enjoyed his company and never once regretted giving up the week's holiday she had intended to spend in Spain with her aunt and uncle to show him around, but she had certainly never expected to hear from him again. He had been a tough, gritty individual with no room for sentimentality in his make-up.

She opened the letter, the words blurring as she trembled in sudden shock.

It wasn't from Tip, but from his lawyers, informing her that she was a beneficiary under the terms of his will, and requesting her to fly out to Texas to the family ranch where the full position would be explained to her.

She sat down, stricken with shock and sadness. Somehow she found it hard to accept that Tip was dead. He had seemed such a vital man, despite his heart condition. He had confided to her in a rare moment of weakness that he had no intentions of dying yet, because he still had too much to do...

'There's that grandson of mine...'

He had shaken his head, and again Natasha had sensed some sort of conflict between the two men. She wasn't a fool. It was easy to see how hard Tip must be to live with. He had his own decided views on everything—many of them uncompromisingly harsh—but then he had lived a harsh life, fighting for most of it to hang on to what he considered to be rightfully his. His grandfather had carved the ranch out of nothing, sometimes quite literally fighting with his bare hands to hold on to it and pass it down through his family.

Allowances had to be made for such men, although she was the first to admit that living with him on a day-to-day basis could never be easy. She had winced sometimes to see and hear how he had treated the staff at his hotel. The American credo might stipulate that all men were equal, but those with money, it appeared, were more equal than those without.

And yet, despite it all, she had liked him. In many ways he had reminded her of her own grandfather, who had died when she was six years old. They had both possessed that same brand of toughness, of hardiness, and of love for their land.

Her sadness at his death increased the greyness of the cold summer's day. She picked the letter up again, studying it idly. Texas . . . Even the word was exciting . . . punchy . . . She couldn't imagine what he had left her, or why. He had not struck her as the overly sentimental type.

Initially, when she had rescued him from the taxi, he had tried to tip her, but the cool hauteur with which she refused his money had made him eye her with speculative interest.

Later, she had suspected that he had deliberately overplayed his weakness on that first occasion, because during the latter part of the week, he never once displayed any of the feebleness that had made it necessary for him to request her support back to his hotel.

Quite how she had come to agree to act as his guide while he was in London she had no real idea. He had told her that originally it had been the intention that his grandson would accompany him, but some last-minute hitch at the ranch had made this impossible, so he had come on alone, and despite his bravado and his loudness he had been lonely.

Yes, that was what had drawn her to him, she recognised. His loneliness. It was a state she had experienced too much to be able to turn her back on it in anyone else.

But to leave her something... It didn't ring true somehow; it was too out of character... No, he had been too shrewd, too deeply enmeshed in his own sense of family and history to leave something to an outsider. That smacked too much of a sentimentality she knew he hadn't possessed.

She couldn't imagine what he had left her... Another frown wrinkled her forehead. Her skin was the colour of cream, and impossible to tan. When she went abroad she spent a fortune on barrier creams, and she had to wear a hat to stop herself from getting sunstroke.

She tapped the letter with one long forefinger. Of course, she could always refuse to go. In that event, her bequest would be forfeit...

It was a rather odd clause to include... There was even a provision for her air fare. She frowned again. She had been quite open with Tip about her financial situation. He knew that...

She blocked off the thought because, since it was associated with her parents' death and the subsequent sale of the farm, she found it painful still.

Suffice it to say that if she did go to Texas she would pay her own way there, and Tip must surely have realised that... *If* she went...she *couldn't* go! She had already decided to spend two of her four weeks' holiday in Spain with her aunt and uncle—she hadn't seen them for over twelve months, and had tentatively been considering Adam's suggestion that she spend the other fortnight with him on a friend's yacht, sailing round the Greek islands.

She ought to go. She owed Tip that much, surely? Or was she using his bequest as an excuse to delay making a decision about her relationship with Adam? In her heart of hearts she knew she was already regretting her promise to join him and his friends. It had been given in a moment of weakness and had left her with a panicky feeling of being pushed, albeit gently, in a direction she wasn't sure she wanted to go.

Now she had the perfect escape route.

Yes, that was the answer. Fate had handed her the perfect excuse. She already knew deep down inside her that Adam wasn't the one for her. This way she could let him know it more tactfully than if she simply handed in her notice and left. She enjoyed her work, but she knew it wasn't taxing her to the full, wasn't making the most use of the university degree she had expended so much time and effort in gaining. After university there had been the fine arts course in Italy, paid for as a twenty-first birthday present by her aunt and uncle. She had enjoyed that, and it had been her entrée into the arty world. London was full of young women like her, she thought in a moment of cynicism. Over-qualified for what they did... If she didn't *look* the way she did, elegant and decorative, Adam would never have hired her, despite her impressive qualifications. She remembered her life in Cheshire and how the farmers' wives had been cherished for their ability to work hard alongside their husbands, rather than for their looks, but even there certain taboos and rules had applied. A woman was supposed to fit in with her husband's life-style rather than develop one of her own. A farmer's wife who wanted to write, or to paint, would have gained scant approval among her peers. In so many ways men made the rules and women lived by them.

She moved restlessly round her small flat, unable to define exactly what was making her feel so restless. Maybe it was an echo of Tip's outrageous tall tales of Texas, with its wide open skies and harsh landscape. It was a land that demanded much from its people, and a land she knew next to nothing about, and yet a land that held some mystical allure for her, which she couldn't totally understand.

Had that long ago ancestress of hers—who had come from the wild freedom of the Russian steppes in the wake of the Tsar Nicholas on his visit to Regency England—given her more than just her vivid colouring?

They had long memories in Cheshire, and her grandfather had told her the tale of the wild Russian woman brought back from London by his ancestor. She had been a serving girl in the retinue of one of the Russian princesses; a free woman who had boldly given up everything she knew to follow the man she loved.

Had she missed the empty wildness of her native land? Had she ached, as Natasha herself sometimes ached, for something more than her life encompassed? Had she known the same wildness of spirit deep down inside her? It was a wildness that Natasha had long ago learned to control, but it was still buried deep inside her: a yearning, an aching for... for what? For freedom? Why did she think she might find that freedom in Texas? Surely she hadn't been foolish enough to fall for Tip's stories? She had travelled enough to know that people were the same wherever one went—their emotions...their hopes...their fears—but still she knew that, despite all her logical analysis, she would go to Texas.

Adam was astounded when she told him.

'You can't mean it!' he expostulated, as they ate a late lunch in a small 'in' restaurant off Bond Street.

'I have to go to find out what he's left me,' she pointed out calmly.

Adam frowned. 'There is that, of course, but it won't be much,' he warned her. 'I know these Texans, Natasha... It's family first, second and third...'

Adam knew little of her life before she came to London, and so she smiled coolly at him, knowing that he had just destroyed any chance there might have been of a more intimate relationship between them. If he knew her so little that he actually thought she could be motivated by greed, then he was most definitely not the man for her.

Force of habit made her keep her thoughts to herself, her smile calm and unrevealing as she listened to him and ate her meal. She waited until they were on the point of leaving before telling him that she had not changed her mind.

'Well, if you go, it means that you will have to leave the gallery,' Adam told her. 'I can't afford to have you missing right now... and there are plenty of other women looking for jobs...'

It was a threat and they both knew it, but Natasha chose not to betray her knowledge.

'I'm sorry, Adam. I have to go... As you say, you can't afford to give me time off right now, so I think it best all round if I hand in my notice.'

He looked stupefied, and she was quite surprised by the sensation of exhilaration and freedom that rushed over her. She had worked at the gallery for two years without realising how much she was beginning to dislike it.

'I suppose you're hoping he's left you enough to mean that you won't have to work,' Adam sneered. 'Or maybe you've got other plans. With looks like yours, you might be able to hook yourself a real-life millionaire while you're out there, is that it?' he suggested crudely. 'Well, be warned, Natasha. Oil prices aren't what they were... and Texan women are pretty tough competition. Money marries money out there...'

She managed to hold on to her temper until after he had gone. She had no wish to quarrel with him, and there was little point in countering his snide suggestions. Let him think what he wished...

A husband, children, a home—yes, these were all things she wanted; but she had no need to sell herself to get them. When she married it would be to a man she could respect, a man whose life she could share, a man who respected her...

Respect? A mirthless smile tugged at her lips. There must be more of that good Cheshire blood in her than she had known... What had happened to love? Or, at twenty-five, was she too old to be chasing after that elusive chimera? She had seen her friends in love, and seen that love fade, only to be reborn again with someone else... Married couples changed partners in a strange and complex dance that left her wary and aloof. She still held true to the old tenets and old ways: marriage was for life... That was how she wanted hers to be. If she couldn't have that, then better not to marry at all.

Once she'd made up her mind to go out to Texas, the whole trip began to take on the air of an adventure, fuelled as much by the fact that her aunt and uncle took a very similar view to her plans as Adam had, as by anything else.

Her aunt complained over the telephone that she no longer understood her; that she had always been such a practical, sensible girl.

Perhaps that was half the trouble—she had been *too* sensible, repressing the zinging love of life and adventure that was such a part of her character, out of a desire to please others rather than herself.

She grieved for Tip, of course; she had liked the old man very much but, as she went sedately about her daily life, making her plans, nothing could quite subdue the bubble of excitement frothing inside her.

Adam accused her of being childish.

'What do you expect to find out there?' he had demanded in a last, vain attempt to prevent her leaving. 'Romance? Love? Do you think the whole state's filled with lean-hipped, laconic cowboy types, just waiting to sweep you off your feet? Is that it?'

Of course she didn't, but the picture he conjured up was an irresistible one, and only added to her determination to go. Sanely and honestly, she didn't know why she was so intent on going; partly it was because of Tip, of course, but there was more to it than that—much, much more.

She was even buying a new wardrobe especially for the trip. The day after she made her decision she had thrown open her wardrobe doors and looked thoughtfully at the silk dresses and neat suits therein, and on a sudden impulse—remembering the jeans of her teenage years—she had gone out scouring the shops for clothes suitable to wear on a Texan cattle ranch.

She didn't know how long she would have to stay; the letter simply stated that there were certain conditions attached to her bequest which were best explained *in situ*. She couldn't begin to work out what they were but, at the end of the day, there was no way anyone could force her to accept either a bequest or conditions she did not want; and with that escape route very much to the forefront of her mind she felt quite comfortable about following the instructions contained in the lawyer's letter.

She bought a round-trip ticket, and booked herself into a Dallas hotel room overnight. She held a current driver's licence, her visa was rushed through and she was assured that there would be no problems in her hiring a car. If, as she suspected from Tip's conversation, the ranch was a long, long way from the nearest town, then she would prefer to drive herself to her ultimate destination rather than rely on others.

Who would own the ranch now? Presumably Tip's grandson; the one who had been refusing to knuckle down and marry as Tip had wanted him to do. 'One grandson—that's all I've got, and he's so damned cussed he won't settle down and start a family,' he had complained to Natasha on more than one occasion, and sometimes in terms earthy enough to bright a faint tinge of colour to her pale skin. Tip was nothing if not frank about his grandson's prowess with the female sex, and Natasha could see that he was more than proud of him, although deploring the fact that he was not prepared to confine his activities to one woman and get down to the all-important business of providing him with great-grandsons.

Oddly for an American, Tip had had no photographs to show her, but from his conversations she had gained the impression that his grandson was cast very much in the mould of the older man. She suspected that, if they met, she wouldn't like him. What was acceptable in an old man of seventy-odd was not so easy to overlook in a much younger male!

Chauvinistic didn't even begin to describe the Travers men, or so it seemed from Tip's description of his own and his grandson's attitudes to life. Arrogance seemed to sit on their shoulders as naturally as their Stetson hats fitted their heads. But, of course, she could be wrong; Tip's grandson could turn out to be very different from the way she visualised him.

She had booked her flight for the end of the week, which left her just about enough time to sort herself out. A visit to her bank provided the necessary currency and traveller's cheques. Like her aunt and uncle, the manager was surprised at what she was planning to do, and she wondered wryly how much of his concern sprang from a regard for her and how much from a regard for her bank balance, for Natasha was a very wealthy woman. Something she preferred to keep quiet about. Tip had wormed the truth out of her, but very few people did.

After her parents' death, her trustees had been approached by a large building concern who wanted to buy the farm land, to put up an estate to service the new town being built locally. Her trustees had agreed and, cautious, careful men that they were, they had looked after her money very well for her during the years of her minority. If she had wanted to, she could quite properly have described herself as a millionairess—something that not even Adam knew.

Initially she had hated to even think about her wealth, because it went hand in hand with her parents' death, and then later as she grew older, she had seen how the world treated those with money, especially young and vulnerable women with money, and so it was something she never mentioned.

She supported several charities, but always anonymously, and for the rest, she preferred to live modestly within her income from her job. The only significant purchase she had made from her inheritance had been her flat, and even that was surprisingly modest in view of her means. She didn't even run a car—it wasn't feasible while living in London. Clothes were her one extravagance, but even then she shopped shrewdly, waiting for the sales, spending her money on one good item and then adding less expensive accessories.

Tip had heartily approved of all this. He had told her, with a frankness that almost made her grit her teeth, that he didn't approve of women inheriting money or property, but that he could see that she was an exception to this rule and that she was obviously a very sensible young woman.

It was ironic to think that he was the very means of her rebelling against that sensibleness, and she chuckled out loud, wondering what he would have thought had he known he was responsible for her altering so much of her way of life.

CHAPTER TWO

NATASHA left London on a cold, windy Saturday morning. It was going to be a long flight, but she was well prepared for it, with a new blockbuster paperback and the minimum of hand luggage, all packed away in a soft roll bag in the same pretty shade of peach as her track suit.

She had chosen the track suit especially to travel in. It was made in a fine lightweight cotton, its padded blouson-jacket top warm enough for the cold London morning and the air-conditioned flight, the thin matching T-shirt underneath it cool enough for the heat of Dallas once she arrived.

She had found a pair of toning cotton boots with a pretty white trim, and for once her hair was not coiled back in an elegant knot, but left to curl freely on to her shoulders.

Her own mirror had told her that she looked completely different from her normal work-a-day elegant self—much more like the teenager who had loved life on her parents' farm. The track suit suited her rangy slenderness, its soft peach colour a startling foil for her dark red hair. Several of the male passengers gave her a second look as she stalked past them with the feline walk she wasn't aware of possessing.

Shaking free of the self-imposed restrictions of her London life had unleashed something elemental and untamed within her, releasing a female power she was not yet aware of. It clung to her as provocatively as the scent of musk; invisible, and yet strong enough to draw the masculine eye and attention.

Luckily, the plane wasn't full, and so she had the advantage of an empty seat in which to place her bag. She settled down for the long flight and opened her book.

Dallas came as something of a disappointment, but she told herself that it was only to be expected that one airport should be much like another.

At Customs, her passport was examined by a tall red-headed man, who hesitated and then said in a soft Texan drawl, 'Miss Ames, you'll find someone waiting to meet you in the Arrivals lounge. Have a nice day!'

Someone had come to meet her? The fatigue of the long flight fell away and she felt a sudden surge of optimism. She had heard about American hospitality, and now it seemed that she was to experience it first-hand.

As she waited for her luggage, she surveyed the exit to the Arrivals hall. Luckily her cases came off almost first. A lone male traveller offered to put them into her trolley, but she refused, her cool smile fending him off. He watched her departing back with a rueful grimace which she didn't see.

The Arrivals hall was seething, and she frowned as she looked hesitantly round it. Someone was waiting for her here, but who? And how on earth was she supposed to recognise them?

In the end, she didn't need to. A hand suddenly gripped her elbow, causing her to spin round in sudden shock.

Cold grey eyes stared down into the wary amber depths of hers, a hard, chiselled male face studying her with acute dislike.

'Natasha Ames.'

It was a statement and not a question, delivered in a thin-lipped drawl that held none of the lazy warmth of the customs officers. An almost hawklike profile; a Stetson worn low over his forehead; glossy, thick, night-black hair...these were the first impressions of the man holding on to her.

She tried to pull free, wincing as she felt the callused pads of his fingers tighten their grip. He was tall enough for her to need to tilt her head right back to look into his face, immediately putting her at a disadvantage. A prickle of atavistic animosity ran through her. Without a word being exchanged she knew that this man didn't like her. She felt it bone-deep in the contact of his flesh on hers; had seen it in that brief clash of eyes.

Who was he, and why had he come to meet her? She had been perfectly happy with her own arrangements for getting out to the ranch!

The strong streak of independence bred in her by her ancestors flared up dangerously, her eyes cold, her voice as brittle and clear as glass as she stood back from him and demanded coolly, 'You seem to have the advantage of me... You appear to know my name, but I'm afraid I don't know yours, Mr...'

Her coldness made as much impact as snow falling on foot-thick ice. He looked down at her, grey eyes boring into her skull, cynicism carved deeply into the lines round his eyes and mouth.

'My grandfather said you were a sassy little
thing... It wasn't often that he made an error of
judgement.' A thin smile twisted his mouth. 'Is that
how *you* would describe yourself, Miss Ames?'

Again that grey-eyed glance slashed across her
face, telling her that *his* description of her would
always be less than flattering.

Fighting against a sudden surge of uneasiness,
she struggled to meet him on equal terms, refusing
to be dominated by his arrogant masculine
demeanour.

'No... no, it isn't,' she told him calmly. 'For one
thing, I'm not exactly little——' Her eyes held his,
warning him that she was not going to allow him
to browbeat her.

'I've just had a long flight here... It's very kind
of you to meet me, but I do have a hotel room
booked, so if you will excuse me.'

Her voice matched his for coldness, she made a
move to walk past him, but he still held on to her
arm, and the force he used to make her stand still
left her short of breath, although she was too angry
and too proud to let him see it.

'Let's get this over with just as quickly as possible, shall we, Miss Ames? You're here to see what
the old man left you, and for no other reason, no
matter how much you might want to play at being
a tourist. My plane is standing by to fly us out to
the ranch... If you'd like to come this way...'

Anger took over. She dug her heels in, resisting
his attempt to draw her forward.

'Now, just a minute... I'm not going anywhere
with you. For one thing, I don't have the faintest
idea who you are, and I...'

'You what?' His voice was soft, but the look he gave her was decidedly ugly. 'Don't go home with strange men? That's not the way the old man told it...'

She had to bite down hard on the words springing to her tongue. Tip had been the type of man to indulge in a little harmless boasting. It was obvious now that this man standing in front of her was his grandson, even though he hadn't introduced himself to her. Who knew what tall tales Tip had taken home with him? Seventy-odd or not, he had still been the sort of man who enjoyed female adulation. She had seen that and been tenderly amused by it, even though she had made it quite clear that their relationship was one of friendship only and she knew that she had won his respect, but even so she did not put it entirely past him to have returned home boasting about his English conquest. He had been that sort of man...

Unlike his grandson, she decided, risking a brief glance at the hard profile angled towards her. This man would never, ever discuss his relationship with women in his life; if indeed there was a woman hardy enough to brave that icy disdain!

The anger that had flared in her died suddenly, her interest piqued by his attitude towards her. What did it matter what he or anyone else here thought about her? Her relationship with Tip had been wholly innocent, and she ought to be amused rather than annoyed that a man as cynical and worldly as this one obviously was could be taken in by an old man, bluffing his way through life. Even so, she was still angry enough to want to taunt him a little.

Looking up at him through dark, curling lashes, she said sweetly, 'Do I look the sort of woman who makes a play for older men?'

Her gibe bounced harmlessly off him, his eyes narrowing in bitter concentration on the upturned oval of her face as he said bitterly, 'Yes...provided he's rich enough to afford you. Gramps told us you worked in an art gallery—where they paid you peanuts. That fancy rig you're wearing didn't come cheap, lady...'

It took her a moment to catch her breath, and by that time he was hurrying her through the Arrivals hall.

What on earth had happened to this man to make him so bitter, so cynical about her sex? He was what...somewhere in his early thirties? Good-looking, if you liked the rough-hewn, domineering type. More than good-looking, she acknowledged with another quick glance at his impassive profile. He was dark enough to possess Indian or Mexican blood; she couldn't remember Tip mentioning anything about either of his son's wives. Women hadn't held much importance in Tip's life, except as the providers of sons and grandsons, and great-grandsons...

'It's very kind of you to come all this way simply to pick me up, Mr...'

The sweet sarcasm of her comment bounced back off him. With a hard sideways look, he told her laconically, 'I didn't... I had to come down to pick up the girls.'

The girls! Wild thoughts of tarty good-time girls joining them on the flight were swiftly banished when he added, 'They're at school here in Dallas, and school's out for the summer now...'

'Oh, I see.' She didn't, of course, but it was becoming a challenge to see if she could actually goad him into some sort of response, and so she added questioningly, 'The girls...they're your daughters?'

She could feel the heat in the sideways glance slashed in her direction, and she had to fight against responding to it.

'My brother's.'

She could almost feel the tight-lipped clenching of his jaw that went with the raw admission. Why should it cause him so much pain to tell her that? She frowned, deep in thought, trying to remember the little Tip had told her about his family. There had been another grandson; he had been killed, like her parents, in a road accident along with his wife. Ah, yes, she remembered it now. Something about a quarrel, but between whom and what about she didn't know.

Tip hadn't mentioned his great-granddaughters at all, but then, of course, they were female...and thus to be easily disregarded.

She frowned again as they walked out across the hot tarmac. Her captor was still holding her arm; standing between her and the hot wind racing across the exposed space, but she didn't delude herself that he was standing so close to her from any gentlemanly concern for her.

This hostility, this almost ferocious dislike of her wasn't something she had bargained for and yet, instead of frightening her, she found it challenging.

Again those callused fingertips brushed her skin, causing a faint frisson of sensation to whirl through her. Without turning to look at him, she knew that he was aware of her sudden shiver, and she hoped that he thought it was caused by dislike. It was rather unnerving to be so aware of him as a man, when quite plainly he loathed and detested the very sight of her.

He must have recognised her from the few photographs Tip had insisted on them having taken together, she mused as they approached an immaculate—although frighteningly small—Cessna aircraft, which brought her back to another matter.

'You still haven't told me your name,' she reminded him when they stopped alongside the plane. Where on earth had it come from, this dangerous desire to goad him until she could see the grey eyes burn with controlled ire?

'Jay—Jay Travers,' he told her laconically. 'I'm sure my grandfather mentioned me to you.'

His mouth twisted oddly over this last cynical statement, and deep down inside her something fluttered in feminine response.

'Oh, yes,' she countered sweetly, determined not to let him see how he affected her. 'But only as "my grandson".'

There, *that* should put him in his place! He struck her as a man so fiercely proud and independent that he would loathe the very thought of being considered a mere adjunct to anyone.

He didn't make any attempt to help her board the small plane, much to her relief. She didn't like the way her thought processes became tangled up when he touched her.

As she entered the small cabin, she saw that it already had two other occupants.

'You found her then, Uncle Jay. Great, now we can go! I'm just dyin' to git back to the ranch...'

'You quit talking like that, Rosalie... You know that Gramps sent us to school so that we could learn to talk properly and become ladies.'

Two voices, one brimful of mischief, the other slightly prim; two identical faces with matching sets of blonde pigtails; two small noses liberally sprinkled with freckles, and two pairs of grey eyes remarkably like those possessed by their uncle.

The girls were twins, and they were studying Natasha with open interest.

'Is this her, then, Uncle Jay? Gramps's fancy-piece?'

A muffled giggle from the silent twin belied the innocence shining out of the clean little-girl face.

Although she fought against showing it, Natasha was appalled. Was that how *all* of Tip's family thought of her? If so, she would have to disabuse them of their false ideas, right away. She opened her mouth to do so, and would have done, if she hadn't caught the faint flicker of fear running over the silent twin's face. She turned her head to see what had frightened her, and realised that Jay was standing behind her, studying the twins with hard implacability.

'Apologise to Miss Ames, Rosalie,' he commanded, thin-lipped. 'That's not the way to treat our guests.'

A bright flush stained the small face, and Natasha felt her heart go out to the child. She was, after all, only repeating what she must have overheard from adults. She wanted to say as much to Jay Travers, but was surprised to discover that she didn't have the courage.

'I'm sorry I was rude, Miss Ames.'

Two pairs of grey eyes watched her uncertainly, and then the irrepressible Cherry burst out, 'If you'd have married Gramps, would that have made you our grandmother? We'd have liked that, wouldn't we, Rose? Gramps was always saying that we needed a woman about the place. I 'spect that's why he brought you out here...'

Natasha could feel the hairs lifting at the back of her neck, and she knew that the sudden tension filling the small enclosed space did not come from her.

What had Cherry said that made Jay go so instantly tense? Whatever it was, *she* was not likely to find out. Besides, she had more pressing matters to attend to right now.

'Cherry, your grandfather and I were friends—nothing more,' she explained as she leaned towards the little girl. 'And he didn't bring me out here, I came because...'

'Because he's left you half the ranch. Yes, we know all about that!'

'Cherry!'

The whip-hard voice cut through the little girl's revelations.

Natasha spun round, her face suddenly milk-white. It *couldn't* be true, Cherry must have misunderstood. She opened her mouth to question Jay, but he was already turning his back on her.

'Time we were taking off... Cherry, please show Miss Ames how to fasten herself into her seat...'

'Just a minute...'

It was too late, he was already disappearing into the nose of the aircraft, and as she subsided into her seat alongside the girls she was dimly aware of Cherry saying placatingly, 'Don't worry, Miss Ames. Uncle Jay is a real good pilot... You'll be quite safe.'

She lay back in her seat and closed her eyes, trembling with shock. Tip *couldn't* have left her half the ranch; it just wasn't possible. The twins must have overheard something and misunderstood the situation... She looked covertly at them. They were what... ten? Nine? Old enough and intelligent enough not to make those kind of mistakes... Something twisted painfully deep inside her. She *had* to have an explanation. She *had* to get off this plane.

She wasn't even aware of struggling to sit up until she felt Cherry tugging sympathetically on her arm.

'It's all right, Miss Ames, really,' the little girl reassured her. 'We'll be there inside an hour. You're quite safe... Rosalie used to hate flying too, didn't you?'

Her sister nodded.

'And driving—especially after Momma and Poppa were killed.' She shuddered tensely, her eyes clouding.

'Gramps told us that your parents died in a car crash just like ours.' Cherry looked at her uncertainly. 'Did they?'

'Yes. Yes, they did. When I was sixteen...'

'And where did you go? What happened to you?'

'I went to live with my aunt and uncle.'

'Just like us with Uncle Jay. He takes care of us now, but he doesn't have a wife, does he, Rose?'

She looked to her twin for corroboration. 'Gramps wanted him to get married. He was always going on about it. "The ranch needs sons"—that's what he used to say...'

'Did he tell you that our great-grandmother was an Indian?'

So that explained the dark hair and olive skin! Natasha gave Cherry a distracted smile, and was on the point of asking her gently if she really should be telling her so much about her family, when Rosalie added, 'She was his second wife. He had another one first... She came from New York, and she was very rich, but she died...'

'Yes, and Gary, her son, quarelled with Gramps because he wanted to sell the ranch, and so Gramps gave him the oil wells. And then he got married again and had another son so that he could leave him the land...'

Tip had mentioned a family feud to her, but she had never pressed him for further details. In Cheshire, people were reticent about their family history. Here in Texas it seemed to be just the opposite.

'Our mummy went away and left us, but Daddy went to get her back——'

'That's when they were killed... They were always fighting, weren't they, Rose? But we miss them a lot...'

There was no mistaking the emotion in those few pitiful words, and Natasha felt her own eyes fill up with tears.

'Gramps said that we needed a woman to love us, and that men don't understand women's things... We thought he meant that Uncle Jay was going to get married...women flock round him like bees round honey...but he don't have no truck with them, does he, Rose? Gramps used to say that he was a mis a...'

'A misogynist,' Natasha told her wryly.

Their conversation was a blend of *naïveté* and sophistication: bits of gossip picked up here and there around the ranch no doubt. Even though Tip had not mentioned them to her, she sensed that they had loved him very deeply, and he had obviously cared for them; cared enough, at least, to know that they needed a woman to share their lives.

'Gramps told us a secret before he died. He made us promise not to tell anyone...'

The grey eyes sparkled, and Natasha knew that she was being begged to question this secret. However, she shook her head; she felt she had already pried far enough into Tip's family history, albeit innocently.

'If it's a secret, that's the way it must stay... Your grandfather wouldn't have told it to you if he wasn't sure you could keep it.'

She felt mean as she watched the excitement die out of their eyes, but she told herself it was for the best. Already in these two girls she sensed a yearning, a reaching out to her, which she suspected stemmed not just from their own need to replace their dead mother, but also from Tip's careful tutoring.

It was no secret that he had wanted Jay to marry, and what better way to coerce him than to enrol the two little girls on his side? A mother for them, a wife for Jay, and a great-grandson for Tip... Oh, yes! He had been a wily old character, Natasha reflected grimly. But none of that could explain Cherry's comment about his will.

There was no way that the man she had known in London would have parted with a single inch of his land to someone outside his family. No, the girls must have overheard something and misinterpreted it. To judge from the reception she had received from Jay, she was already marked down as a first cousin to a fortune-hunter, and no doubt the girls had picked up some derogatory remark made about her by their uncle and woven their own reason for it.

It had been dusk when she arrived at Dallas; now it was fully dark. Not the dark of London that she was used to, but the dense blackness of the wide open spaces, illuminated only by the stars, surely far more brilliant here than they had ever seemed at home?

Despite her tiredness, despite the shock of Jay's hostility and the twins' revelations, somewhere deep down inside her that tiny flicker of excitement still burned. Idiotically, since she was in a fully enclosed plane, she felt as though she could almost smell the hot, dry scent of the land, as though its lure and magic were already weaving their spell around her.

She wondered how close to the Rio Grande the ranch actually was. Tip hadn't said, although he had said that the ranch had survived in the early years because it had its own water supply that didn't dry out, even in the longest drought.

Suddenly she felt the plane start to drop. At her side, Cherry said reassuringly, 'Don't worry, it won't be long now.'

As she glanced out of the window, Natasha had a confused impression of rows of oil derricks, and flat, sandy earth, illuminated by the huge flood-lights on top of the derricks.

'Those are Uncle Pete's oil wells,' Rosalie told her matter-of-factly.

'They used to be,' Cherry corrected her. 'Gramps said that most of 'em belong to Uncle Sam now.'

Natasha hid a small smile as she heard Rosalie saying curiously, 'But we don't have an Uncle Sam...'

'No! Gramps meant the government—silly!'

The plane banked drunkenly, and ahead of them Natasha could see the long, brightly lit airstrip. And then they were going down, bumping gently on the tarmac, slowing to a halt.

Cherry and Rosalie busied themselves unfasten-ing their seat-belts and collecting their things as matter-of-factly as though they might have got off the tube. But to these children flying was a part of their lives.

Natasha followed them as they moved towards the exit. Jay Travers came to join them, his Stetson still rammed down on his head. Did he always wear it? she wondered. He had struck her as being too cynical and too worldly to constantly parody the cowboy image. She glanced again at his worn jeans and dusty boots. There had been other men wearing Stetsons at the airport, but they had all been dressed in executive suits, or immaculate western outfits...

'I'm a working rancher, Miss Ames,' she heard him saying behind her as he reached out to open the door. 'I'm sorry if my clothes aren't what you're used to, but out here time is money...'

'And I wasn't worth the time and effort it would have taken you to get changed,' Natasha said sardonically, holding back any further comment when she saw how intently the girls were listening to them.

Jay, it seemed, had no inhibitions.

'Gramps was right about one thing,' he agreed. 'You sure are quick on the uptake...'

The way he said it, it wasn't a compliment, and Natasha felt an angry flush sear her skin as she followed the two girls down on to the airstrip.

It was surprisingly cold, and then she remembered that this land came pretty close to desert conditions, and that the temperature would drop dramatically at night.

As the girls raced over to the waiting vehicle, Natasha hesitated. Her cases were still in the plane, and she suspected it would be unwise to rely on Jay's chivalry to bring them for her. As she paused, a chilly breeze raised goose-bumps on her exposed arms.

'You'd better go get in the truck. Didn't Gramps tell you anything about conditions out here? Or were you so eager to come and claim your dues that you forgot?'

Her brief softening toward him, born of his sudden appreciation of her shivers, died as she listened to his sarcastic words.

'My luggage is still on board the plane,' she told him, ignoring his taunt.

'I'll see to that. Go join the girls.'

Much as she longed to ignore his command, she knew it would be foolish to simply stand around and shiver, while she waited for him to bring her cases.

The vehicle he had described as 'the truck' was huge. It *was* a truck, in that there was an open section at the back, but as Cherry opened the door for her she gasped to see the luxurious interior, with its front and rear bench seats and sophisticated bank of equipment.

'Some truck,' she muttered under her breath, causing the girls to giggle.

'Uncle Jay uses it when he's driving around the ranch,' Cherry explained. 'It has full radio contact with the ranch so that he can keep a check on what's going on, and these seats make up into a bed in case he has to stay out overnight. It's real neat, isn't it?'

Natasha had to agree that it was, although her slightly puritan Cheshire soul protested a little at its opulent luxury. Her father had driven round his farm in a battered old Land Rover, with the hardest bench seats in the world and an antiquated form of heating that constantly belched out putrid and polluted air. It had been practically held together with pieces of string and odd bits of wire! In Cheshire, farmers were a thrifty, frugal lot who did not believe in expending money on new equipment while the old was still in working order.

Luckily the back seat was wide enough for her to be able to wedge herself alongside the girls. There was no way she was going to sit next to Jay and listen to more of his acerbic comments.

It took twenty minutes to drive back to the homestead, along one of the straightest bitumen roads Natasha had ever seen, and at a speed that had her clutching the sides of her seat as she tried to control her start of terror.

'It's all right, Uncle Jay isn't going to hit anything,' Cherry assured her kindly, calling out, to Natasha's chagrin, 'Can't you slow down some? Natasha is scared...'

'We used to be scared, too, when our folks were first killed, but Gramps said that the only way to get over falling off a horse was to climb right back on again.'

Yes, she could just hear him saying it too, Natasha thought wryly.

'Don't worry, I'll let you hold my hand. That will make you feel a lot better... Uncle Jay always lets me hold his when I'm scared...'

So the man was human, after all. It came as something of a shock, and she couldn't resist sneaking a glance at his rigid profile.

In the darkness of the truck she could just about make it out. While she was studying him he turned his head abruptly, as though sensing her scrutiny, and immediately she was aware of his leashed tension and resentment. Surely the fact that she had befriended his grandfather and had been left some small token in remembrance of that friendship could not be responsible for this almost savage sense of hostility she sensed in him?

Uncertainly, like someone probing an aching tooth, she examined her own feelings. It was unheard of for her to react so strongly to a man on such a short acquaintance... What had happened to her notorious coldness, so much bemoaned by other men? What had happened to the cool hauteur behind which she habitually hid her real feelings?

'We're almost there now.' Cherry's excited comment distracted her and she followed the little girl's pointing finger. 'Look, those are the breeding pens and the cattle sheds,' she announced importantly. 'Uncle Jay is trying to develop a new strain of Brahmin cattle, that will give leaner meat. He...'

'I'm sure Miss Ames isn't interested in any of that, Cherry.' Jay's ice-cold voice cut across the little girl's excited chatter, and Natasha felt her resentment of him harden into something deeper.

If he wasn't concerned with her feelings, surely he might have considered those of his niece? Or was he like his grandfather... did female members of the human race have no importance at all in his scheme of things?

It was cool, prim Rosalie who put the final seal on what Natasha felt was already promising to become a disastrous decision by saying virtuously, 'Gramps used to say that Uncle Jay would have been better off breeding sons than wasting his time trying to breed a new type of cattle...'

'That's enough!'

Instant silence consumed the interior of the truck. Natasha found she was wishing herself a thousand miles away from Texas, and most especially from the man driving this vehicle. She had come out here with such high hopes, such a feeling of adventure, and within a few short hours he had managed to destroy all of that and replace it with...

With what? Hostility? Fear? Compassion for his two poor nieces—and any other woman unfortunate enough to come within his sphere... Resentment against Tip for putting her in such a position in the first place, and other alien emotions she couldn't even begin to understand.

There had been that frisson of sensation when he had touched her, for instance. That momentary need to know what he would look like with his mouth softened by passion, his eyes hot instead of cold. That terrifying second when she had looked at him and read bitter loneliness in his eyes and almost ached to reach out and smooth it away...

She was imagining things, she told herself. She was suffering from jet-lag. People did the strangest things under its influence. Yes...yes, that was it. She heaved a faint sigh of relief as the truck suddenly stopped. She had been so deeply engrossed in her worrying thoughts that she hadn't realised that they had pulled up in front of what must be the main entrance to the house.

As she stared at it, she caught her breath on a sudden surge of pleasure. It had been built in the Spanish style, which she recognised from trips to Andalucia: long and low, with white walls and a veranda, around which was entwined what she very much suspected must be bougainvillaea.

Another veranda ran round the second storey, with shuttered windows obviously opening out on to it.

'Come on, Miss Ames, we're here!' Cherry tugged on her arm. Natasha shook herself free on her sudden and instinctive sense of homecoming and followed the girls outside.

'Go on into the house. Dolores, our house-keeper, has prepared a room for you, Miss Ames.'

'Uncle Jay...'

The twins' protest was ignored as he swung down from the truck and strode away from them.

'I've got work to do, kids, and it's way past your bedtime... See you in the morning.'

Did that apply to her, too? If so, she ought to be relieved. She was so tired that she could have stretched out on the hard packed earth and dropped straight off to sleep!

'I suppose he's going down to the cow barns. Come on, let's get inside.'

It was Cherry who took charge, pushing open the heavy door and calling out, 'Dolores, we're home!'

The Mexican woman who came in answer to her summons was smiling broadly. She hugged both girls and then turned to look at Natasha, her smile fading abruptly, as she said coolly, 'You'll be wanting to go to your room, Miss Ames. I'll have one of the girls bring you a tray up... Jay said to tell you that breakfast will be at eight, and the lawyer will be here at nine. Tomas will see to your bags. If you'll just come with me.'

What had she done to provoke this degree of antipathy from Tip's staff? Too proud to show how hurt she was by the woman's attitude, she trailed tiredly behind her as she mounted the elegant double-banistered stairs.

'Jay said to put you in the guest suite—for the time being...'

Why was it that those last few words should have such an ominous ring to them? Natasha wondered, as Dolores paused and pushed open one of the many doors leading off the galleried landing.

In London, she had looked forward with hope and anticipation to being asked to stay on for a brief time, but now... Now she was half wishing she had never come, she admitted, as she stepped past Dolores and into her room.

She was left alone to explore it. It was certainly very elegant: not just a bedroom, but a bedroom, a sitting-room and her own private bathroom.

It was decorated in a style that Natasha found slightly pretentious, and not suited to the beautiful simplicity of the Spanish-style house. The furniture was too modern, the pale Nile-green leather settee not in keeping with the building. Her bed was swathed in flimsy printed silk covers, where she would have instinctively chosen a heavily carved Spanish bed and covered it with one of the beautiful heritage quilts she had seen in a display of American goods in Harrods, or perhaps even an Indian or Mexican woven spread. Certainly, she would never have chosen the bedroom's delicate pseudo-French gilt and white trappings.

At home in Cheshire, the farmhouse had been furnished with sturdy heirlooms collected over the generations, each one suited to its purpose and its background. Here she found her surroundings jarred on her, so out of step was the décor with the exterior and the ambience of the house.

Who had been responsible for choosing them? Not a man—they were too flimsy, too delicate for that. They spoke of a woman who loved luxury; a woman who despised the sturdy building that was her home...

She was getting fanciful again, Natasha told herself. For all she knew, Tip might have commissioned interior designers to decorate and furnish this suite.

She was in the bathroom freshening up when she heard her door open. When she returned to her sitting-room she discovered a pot of fragrant coffee and a generous plate of sandwiches waiting for her, along with her luggage.

She poured some of the coffee and ate a couple of sandwiches, stifling her yawns, as she started to make an attempt to unpack. She had to give it up half-way through, overcome by intense exhaustion. A shower and then bed, she decided sleepily. That was what she needed now...

CHAPTER THREE

'WAKE up, Miss Ames. It's well after seven, and Dolores will be mad as fire if you're late for breakfast.'

The voices were familiar, but the room wasn't. Cautiously, Natasha opened both eyes properly.

Of course, Texas... She was in Texas!

This morning the twins were dressed in dungarees and checked shirts, their hair in pony-tails and not plaits.

'Why don't you try calling me Natasha?' she suggested sleepily. 'Miss Ames makes me sound like a schoolteacher. Now then, which of you is which?'

'You can always tell, because Rosalie has a mole just there,' Cherry informed her helpfully, pointing out the small dark mark on her sister's throat.

'I'll go down and tell Dolores you're on your way.' Rosalie slid off the bed and made for the door.

The events of the previous day came crowding back, and unconsciously Natasha sighed.

'Don't worry,' Cherry consoled her. 'Me and Rosalie like you...'

Natasha fought to control her feelings. The girls had been quick to pick up on her misery... too quick, perhaps. It was on the tip of her tongue to ask Cherry why Jay was so antipathetic towards her, but she swallowed her words. She was not going to use the girls in that way. If she really needed to know, then she must ask Jay himself...

But would he tell her? She shrugged the thought aside, pushing back the bedclothes and sliding out of bed.

'Oh, my, that's a real pretty nightgown!' Cherry exclaimed. 'We wear pyjamas.' She wrinkled her nose. 'Uncle Jay doesn't wear anything at all, and we aren't allowed to go into his bedroom in the morning... He always gets up too early anyway.'

'We used to go into Ma and Pa's. That was a long time ago, though... before they started fighting. Before we came to live back here...'

Natasha gave a small start. She had assumed that the girls had been born and brought up on the ranch, but before she could say anything Cherry went on, 'You'll have to hurry. It used to take Ma hours to get ready. That was one of the things that made Daddy real wild. He said she didn't need to get herself all gussied up for living on the ranch. She never wanted to live here. We did, though. Our mother was like you... She came from England.'

Downstairs, a bell rang imperiously.

'That's the breakfast bell. You've got half an hour,' Cherry told her, sliding off the bed. 'I'd better go down.'

So the twins' mother had been English, Natasha reflected as she quickly showered and started to dress. Tip had never mentioned that... but then, why should he?

She wondered uncertainly on what she should wear. To judge from the girls' appearance, jeans would be the order of the day; but she was supposed to be meeting Tip's lawyer to be told the nature of his bequest, and somehow jeans seemed too unbusinesslike for such a meeting.

Old habits die hard, Natasha reflected rather wryly. American laywers were not like their British counterparts—even the most casual watcher of American TV had to be aware of that, but even so she found herself donning a tailored, charcoal-grey skirt and its complementary white silk shirt.

It was one of the few formal outfits she had packed, thinking she might wear it for shopping in Dallas, should she get the chance. It had a matching unlined jacket in the same charcoal-grey, with a shadowed white line forming large checks, and she had bought it in a fit of extravagance.

The grey skirt emphasised the slenderness of her hips and the length of her legs. There wasn't time for her to coil her hair into a chignon, so she compromised by taking it off her face with two mother-of-pearl combs she had found in a small antiques shop in Knightsbridge.

A touch of lip gloss and just enough mascara to darken her long lashes and she was ready to go downstairs and face the world... But was she ready to face Jay?

She ignored the treacherous little voice that asked her the question and hurried downstairs.

Luckily, one of the twins appeared in the hallway at just the right moment to show her the way to the large, sunny room where the table was set for breakfast.

Dolores looked up as they walked in, her eyebrows lifting slightly as she saw Natasha's formal outfit.

'I believe I'm supposed to be seeing Tip's lawyers this morning. At home, we tend to dress rather formally for such events, and I'm afraid old habits die hard.'

Despite her friendly explanation and the smile she gave the Mexican housekeeper, she got no response other than a cool glance from wary brown eyes.

'Uncle Jay's already had his breakfast and gone out to see the stock,' Rosalie told her, correctly interpreting her hesitant glance towards the door.

She ought to have been ashamed of herself for being so relieved, but she was the first to admit that she wasn't at her best first thing in the morning, and the thought of having to cope with the barbed innuendoes of her reluctant host, while still coping with the strain of jet-lag, was less than appealing.

'Sit down here, next to me,' Rosalie invited, pulling out a chair. 'We're having waffles this morning. You'll love them . . .'

The only thing she wanted was a cup of freshly brewed coffee . . . several cups, Natasha amended as she caught the scent from the coffee-pot Dolores brought to the table.

Despite the fact that Dolores was being anything but friendly, Natasha said hesitantly, 'I believe I'm to see Tip's lawyer at nine. When he arrives . . .'

She had been going to ask if someone could let her know, but Dolores anticipated her, saying flatly, 'He's already here. He's been here for the last four days.'

Whether the disapproval in her voice applied only to her, or to the lawyer as well, Natasha couldn't tell.

'He had breakfast with Jay. They had things to discuss. You're to meet them in the den at nine. I'll show you where it is.'

Refusing to share their waffles, Natasha listened to the girls' excited chatter, as she helped herself to more coffee.

Now and again their conversation betrayed a certain loneliness and sense of isolation. There were several mentions of school events at which their family had not been present. And, although it was obvious that they adored Jay, Natasha sensed that they were also a little in awe of him.

At eighty forty-five she excused herself, carrying her used cup through to the kitchen.

She saw that Dolores was surprised to see her there, and obviously even more surprised when she asked if there was anything she could do to help before going up to her room to check on her appearance before her meeting with the lawyer.

'There's no call for any guests around here to do chores,' was Dolores's curt response. 'Jay employs plenty of staff to take care of that...'

Feeling very much as though she had been put firmly in her place as unwanted guest, Natasha retreated. What on earth had she done to merit this hostility? Surely it couldn't just be because Tip had made her a small bequest? But families could be very clannish, very possessive over what they considered to be theirs.

Sighing faintly, she went back to the sunny breakfast-room.

It overlooked the back of the house and an enclosed patio adorned with tubs of brilliantly coloured plants, its white walls covered in creepers,

a small fountain playing in an ornate round pool,
very Spanish in style.

Through the wrought-iron gate set in the wall she
could see a sweep of lawn and the blue glimmer of
what she guessed must be a swimming pool.
Perhaps later on the twins would take her on a tour
of the grounds.

Tip had spent more time boasting about how his
forebears had carved out the ranch from nothing
than describing the house itself to her. It had come
as a pleasant surprise to discover it was such a
gracious building, and she thought she detected a
woman's touch in the pretty enclosed courtyard
beyond the breakfast-room windows.

Upstairs in her own room she checked on her
hair and re-applied fresh lip gloss.

At five to nine she went downstairs again and,
almost as though she had been waiting for her,
Dolores appeared in the hall, gesturing to Natasha
to follow her.

Several doors led off the large, tiled hallway, but
the one Dolores opened for her was tucked away
right at the back, almost under the arch of the
stairs.

At home, she supposed it would have been described as a library or study, Natasha thought as
she stepped into a surprisingly large room and
studied it in silence. Here, though, it was called a
'den', and she could see why. It was more the lair
of man without the trappings of civilisation than
the retreat favoured by men like Adam who liked
to surround themselves with luxury and art.

Here the walls had been left in their natural
whitewashed state. A huge, dark Spanish wood

bookcase took up one wall, its shelves full of
leather-bound volumes, and what looked like
paperbacks, as well as piles of stacked magazines.
Over the open fireplace was an ancient musket, and
alongside it on the same wall, a gun-rack, pad-
locked with a heavy chain. Two enormous leather
couches in oxblood faced one another across a
woven Mexican rug.

A shaft of brilliant sunlight fell across the
enormous desk. The room smelled of leather and
oil, and was so essentially masculine that Natasha
immediately felt an intruder in it.

To her surprise it overlooked the same patio that
ran outside the breakfast-room. A shuttered french
window stood open, and through it she could hear
men's voices.

Gradually, as she waited, other sounds impinged
on her senses: the whirr of the old-fashioned ceiling
fan, the lowing of cattle, bird song and the soft
splash of the fountain—all sounds that somehow
softened the harsh masculinity of her surroundings.

There were several paintings grouped on one wall:
all of cattle, all very stylised, and next to them what
she realised must be an aerial view of the ranch and
outbuildings. Behind the desk was a bank of filing
cabinets. She was just stepping forward to examine
the paintings at closer quarters, when she saw the
two men outside the french door.

As he had been the previous day, Jay was clad
in faded blue jeans and a checked cotton shirt. His
boots were covered in red dust; as he came inside
he removed his Stetson, and she saw that the same
dust had darkened his skin.

As he came in he brought with him the hot, acrid smell of cattle, and the disturbing, musky scent of his own body.

The man behind him was wearing similar clothes, although he was neither quite as tall or as broad as Jay, and his hair was greying at the temples. Unlike Jay, though, he did give her a faint smile.

'I'm glad you let me come in this way,' he was saying ruefully to Jay. 'I don't think Dolores would have taken too kindly to us tracking red dust across the kitchen floor. I think she must have been the only human being I've ever met who could actually make your grandfather toe the line...'

'No one could make Gramps do that,' Jay corrected curtly. 'He just let her think she could because it made life easier all around. Even after Doc Reilly told him to quit smoking and drinking, he used to come in here and help himself to the supplies he kept locked away in his filing cabinet.'

'Didn't you try to stop him?'

'I tried, but in my book a man has a right to choose the way he wants to live, or wants to die.'

The older man broke off their conversation and turned to Natasha.

'I'm sorry, we still haven't been introduced, have we? I'm Harvey Goldstein, Tip's lawyer. And you, of course, must be Natasha... Your photographs didn't do you justice, did they, Jay?'

A non-committal grunt was the other man's only response, and Natasha knew she was flushing, not because of the compliment she had been paid, but because Jay was so obviously contemptuous of it, and of her.

'You obviously received my letter...'

'Yes, yes. It came as something of a shock. Of course, I knew that Tip had a heart condition, but I...I liked him a lot...'

A cynical sound behind her stopped her, her colour deepening. She ached to turn round and tell the man standing behind her how difficult she found this situation. She had not asked to come here, after all; and he should be able to appreciate that, much as she had liked Tip, she found it hard to express a fictitious depth of sorrow at his death. It *had* been a shock, and she *had* been sorry, but to deliver more than the conventional platitudes was impossible in view of his own hostility towards her. Had he been a different type of man, she might have been able to express her enjoyment of Tip's company and salty wit, or to open up to him and tell him that she knew what it was to lose a deeply loved member of one's family—how alone it left one feeling, how frightened and insecure—but she doubted if this man had been frightened of anything in his life. And so she was left feeling that whatever she tried to say would be inadequate.

'Well, he sure liked *you*,' Harvey Goldstein told her. 'Look, why don't we all sit down? And perhaps Dolores would bring us some coffee, Jay?'

Now she recognised the legal mind in him, despite the jeans and casual attire, and she found herself subsiding into a chair, and even risking a coolly polite smile in Jay's direction as he asked her if she wanted anything else to drink.

'Coffee suits me fine.'

The antipathy between them must have been very apparent, because when Jay left the room to get their coffee, Harvey said quietly, 'All this has been very hard for Jay. He thought the world of his grandfather, and...'

He broke off as Jay came back into the room.

'Dolores will be in with the coffee in five minutes. Let's get on with it shall we, Harvey?'

He was the rudest, most uncivil man she had ever met, Natasha seethed, fighting to control her ire at his attitude towards her.

Harvey cleared his throat.

'Well, Natasha, you know from my letter that you were mentioned in Tip's will...'

'Of course she does, Harvey. What else would bring her hot-foot out here, eager to collect the reward for all her hard work? What did you do when you went to bed with him... close your eyes and ignore the fact that he was seventy-five years old?'

Natasha was appalled. She had suspected before that Jay thought that she and Tip might have been lovers, but she had never dreamed he would voice such thoughts—especially in front of someone else...

She stood up, barely aware of pushing her chair away, or of the way she trembled, her face milk-white, her eyes a brilliant tawny-gold as rage rushed through her.

'That's not true! Your grandfather and I were never lovers, whatever he might have told you...'

'He told us nothing,' came the grim response, 'but some things speak for themselves. Why else would he leave you one half of this ranch? Why else would he hand over to a complete stranger the very thing he spent his whole life protecting for his family? What the hell did you give him? It couldn't

just have been the softness of your body. There
must have been something else... What was it? The
promise of another son? Was that it?'

'Jay!' Harvey Goldstein's voice cut across his
impassioned speech in stern warning.

The shock of what she had just heard made
Natasha subside back into her chair, her whole body
shaking. She was dimly aware of the door opening
and Dolores coming in with a laden tray of coffee.
She was also aware of Harvey clearing a space on
the cluttered desk so that she could put down her
tray, but these things barely impinged upon her
awareness. She was still grappling with the enormity of her shock. Tip *couldn't* have done that! He
couldn't have willed half the ranch to her! He had
barely known her. And even in that one short week
she *had* known him, she had felt overwhelmingly
that he was a man who put his family first and
foremost. A man for whom family loyalties and ties
took precedence above all else. A man who would
never will so much as an inch of his land away from
those who shared his own blood.

It must all be some terrible joke... some ma-
cabre folly conjured up by malign fate. It *couldn't*
be true! The shock of what she had just heard far
outweighed her anger at Jay's denunciation of her.
Indeed, she could almost appreciate why he had
made it. In his shoes... but she *wasn't* in his shoes...

'You didn't know?' Harvey was watching her
narrowly. 'Tip made no intimation?'

'Nothing!' Her voice shook. 'He said nothing. I
never...'

'Oh, very clever...' Jay's sneer broke through
her shock. 'Very pretty and innocent, but it won't

wash. My grandfather spent his life building up this ranch, developing and protecting it. He would never have left any part of it to you without good reason...'

'Jay, let me tell her the full terms of Tip's bequest,' Harvey intervened quietly.

Turning to Natasha he said patiently, 'Tip has left you a full half-share in the land and the cattle as well as the house, provided you live here on the ranch for at least six months out of every twelve. Jay here is to remain in control of all policy decisions concerning the ranch. He has appointed both of you as the twins' joint legal guardians...'

He paused, and Natasha managed to stammer, 'Buthowcouldhedothatwithouttellingme? How...'

'Never mind how. He did it,' Jay told her grimly. 'Tell her the rest, Harvey.'

'Briefly, these are the terms of Tip's will, but in consideration of you forfeiting all the rights contained in it, Jay is prepared to make you an immediate payment of two million dollars.'

An awesome silence filled the room; even the fan seemed to stop whirring, although Natasha knew that it had not. The silence came from within her and it was a silence compounded of shock and pain.

What was happening to her was ridiculous; it was like something out of a singularly unenterprising novel; it was unreal... Only it wasn't any of those things, because it *was* real and it *was* happening, and she was feeling this appalling combination of pain and anger that deprived her of breath and left her feeling as though her whole world had been turned upside down.

When it righted again she was left with only two burning thoughts. The first was *why* had Tip done this to her... a woman who was almost a complete stranger to him? And the second was that if it took her the rest of her life to do it, she was going to show Jay how wrong he was in his savage condemnation of her. Before she had finished with him he would be grovelling before her in abject apology; he would be down on his hands and knees begging her for forgiveness.

A red mist swirled in front of her eyes, carrying her away on a dangerous flood of rage, and before it could retreat she heard herself saying passionately, 'Only two million dollars! What sort of fool do you take me for? No, I'm staying...'

She almost took back her hot words when she saw the fierce rage heating those cold grey eyes, but pride armed her and wouldn't let her down. Tip must have had a reason for what he had done, she told herself stoutly. She wouldn't discover what that reason was by running away. Maybe Jay Travers could terrify other people into doing what he wanted, but he would soon discover that *she* didn't allow herself to be dictated to by *any* man.

'Think carefully, Natasha,' Harvey Goldstein urged her calmly. 'Two million dollars is one hell of a lot of money. You could live anywhere in the world on that...' He made a small grimace. 'Texas isn't the best place in the world to live, no matter what Tip might have told you, and ranch life is hard on women...'

She had known all along that Harvey would be on Jay's side, and now he was confirming it. Her mouth compressed bitterly. Did they think she was a complete fool? This ranch—the land alone was worth much more than four million dollars, but that didn't matter. She wondered what they would say if she told them that right at this minute she had almost as much in her bank account in sterling as they were offering her. She toyed with the idea of telling them just for the pleasure of seeing the shock hit their eyes and then she closed her mind to the temptation.

If Tip, who had known of her financial status, had not seen fit to mention it, then neither would she. There was more to this than a simple bequest; even if she and Tip *had* been lovers, she knew he would hardly have rewarded her so generously for the gift of her body. And as it was they hadn't even been more than very casual friends. So why... Why had he done it? She wondered about his mental state at the time he made his will and then dismissed the idea, knowing that, had there been any doubts to cast upon it, Jay Travers would already have cast them.

Tip had appointed her co-guardian of the twins along with Jay. That, in a way, concerned her more than his bequest of the land and the cattle, because it hinted to her that he had felt there might be something lacking in Jay's care of them. The land, the money, these she could have turned her back on; but the twins...

Face it, she told herself sardonically, you want to stay, and not just because the twins could fill an empty space in your life. You want to stay because you want to prove to Jay Travers just how wrong he is!

Yes, it would give her a great deal of pleasure to show Jay that he wasn't the all-knowing, all-invincible character he thought himself to be.

Now, at least Dolores's antipathy, and Jay's, too, was explained. She doubted *she* would have welcomed with open arms someone who was threatening to take over half of what she had thought of as hers. But that didn't excuse Jay's horrible insinuations about the nature of her relationship with Tip...

She studied him for a second, and then asked, 'Did Tip *tell* you he and I were lovers?'

'He didn't need to.' The harshness of his voice almost made her wince. 'There's no way he'd have handed over half of this place to you for any other reason.'

'No.' She smiled delicately at him, suddenly hating him with almost as much vigour as he seemed to hate her. How dared he make such ill-informed judgements about her? How dared he denigrate and insult her?

'What about if he had grave doubts about his only grandson's worthiness to inherit his land...'

There was a moment's stunned silence, and then she watched the slow tide of red creep up over the dark skin, and the grey eyes turn murderous with fury.

'Why, you...'

'Jay, calm down! If Natasha is serious about fulfilling the terms of Tip's will, the two of you will be living side by side. You'll have to find a way to get along...

'Lawyers... Goddamn you, Harvey! But then, it isn't your problem is it? You don't have to live with it—with *her*. Get her out of here before I do something that'll send me to the electric chair...'

Much as she ached to defy him and stay, Natasha allowed Harvey to escort her out of the room.

'I'm sorry about that, but naturally Jay's very upset. He's lived and breathed this ranch all his life, and for Tip to calmly hand over half of it to a complete stranger... Are you sure you won't consider taking the money instead?'

'If I did, would I still retain my co-guardianship of the girls?' Natasha asked him testingly.

Harvey paused for a moment and then shook his head. 'No. I don't know why Tip put in that clause, but Jay doesn't consider that you'd be...the right kind of influence on them...'

'Why not? Because he thinks I slept with his grandfather?'

When there was no reply, save for a very embarrassed look from the lawyer, she shrugged carelessly. 'Anyway, it doesn't matter. I'm staying and there's no way Jay can stop me... Is there?'

Again he shook his head.

'No, but he can make it very unpleasant for you to stay,' he warned her, 'and I suspect he will. Way back, Jay has Indian blood in his veins, and no one can hold on to a grudge like an Indian.'

'Are you warning me, Harvey, or threatening me?' Natasha asked him softly with a mock-sweet smile.

As she watched him back off she felt slightly sorry for him. He was, after all, only carrying out his instructions. Nevertheless, she thought it best to make it plain right from the start that she wasn't going to be easy to push around.

So Jay could make life hard for her, could he? Well, she had had life hard before—and she had survived...

CHAPTER FOUR

'ARE you going to stay and look after us, like Gramps wanted?'

The twins had arrived upstairs in Natasha's room shortly after lunch.

Much to her relief, Jay hadn't put in an appearance at that meal, although it was obvious from Dolores' manner that she knew about what had happened in the den, and also that she heartily disapproved of it.

'Would you like me to?' Natasha probed. Now that her temper had cooled, she was able to take a far more dispassionate view of the whole extraordinary affair. She couldn't even begin to understand why Tip had left such an out-of-character will, and she suspected that, had Jay treated her with courtesy and kindness, she would have quite happily renounced all her rights under Tip's bequest and gone straight home to London.

As it was...as it was, she had virtually committed herself to spending six months out of every twelve in this alien, hostile place, where even the staff looked upon her as an interloper, a fortune-hunter. Did they *all* think that she had earned her bequest by sleeping in Tip's bed? If it hadn't been so ludicrously out of character that she should even consider behaving in such a way, she might have been hurt. As it was, all she could feel was a vast enormity of astonishment, mingled with a pain that sprang from the unwanted knowledge that there was no one close enough to her to share her feelings. No one who knew her in the way that a parent or sibling could have known her and could have shared her rejection of the role cast for her.

The last time she had felt so aware of her aloneness had been in the early months after her parents' death; and the deep intensity of her feelings then came back to haunt her now. She looked at the twins and remembered that they too had lost their parents; that they had an uncle, who was both remote and, it seemed, incapable of making rational and fair judgements of his fellow human beings. Through pride and anger she had already committed herself to staying at the ranch. The twins . . .

'Yes, we do want you to stay,' Cherry told her, interrupting her thoughts. 'We like you, don't we, Rosalie?' She turned to her more silent twin for corroboration. 'Gramps said we would—that was our secret—that he had chosen you specially to look after us. Uncle Jay never has time to come to PTA meetings or anything like that . . . He never takes us out of school for treats like the other kids' folks do. He never has time.'

'You could be our sort of adopted Mom, couldn't she, Rosalie?'

As Natasha saw Rosalie's confirmatory smile, a warm tide of pleasure filled her. Stupidly perhaps in the circumstances, she had wanted to stay . . . had needed an excuse to back up the decision she had made in the heat of the moment, and now she had it. Perhaps it was her Russian blood that wouldn't allow her to back down from a fight. A fight? She grimaced a little to herself. Well, it would certainly be that . . .

To fulfil the terms of Tip's will she had to spend six months out of every twelve actually living at the ranch, and she suspected that Jay was not going to go out of his way to make those six months easy for her.

Still, she had as much right to be here as him. Her chin tilted, and she ignored the truthful inner voice that objected to that statement. She had no real moral right to be here. It was only because of Tip's will that she was . . .

She frowned, pleating the fine skin between her dark brows. She still couldn't understand *why* Tip had made such a will. She couldn't understand it at all. But there must have been some reason for it.

Had he had doubts about his grandson's ability to run the ranch? But no, that couldn't be the reason; after all, what did *she* know about cattle breeding? So why, then? Because he had been concerned about the lack of a female influence in the lives of his great-granddaughters? No, that didn't quite ring true . . .

She might only have known Tip for a week, but during that week she had recognised the essence of the man. Shrewd and slightly calculating would have been the way she would have described him if asked . . . certainly not a sentimentalist. The more she thought about that will, the more convinced she became that Tip had had a definite purpose in doing what he had. But what was that purpose?

Perhaps if she stayed here long enough she might find out ... Perhaps ... Perhaps that was what Tip had wanted all along. For her to stay here. But why?

'We're going out riding. Want to come with us?'

'Well, I'd certainly like to come down and watch,' Natasha temporised. It had been a long time since she had last been on the back of a horse, and she knew that in this part of the States they rode with a different type of saddle from the one she had been used to. She hadn't brought any proper riding gear with her, but she had her jeans ...

'Just let me get changed into something more suitable, and I'll come down with you. Do you both have your own ponies?' she asked, leaving the door open so that they could talk, as she walked through into her bedroom.

'Yes, Uncle Jay bought them for us for our last birthday. Palaminoes ...'

Natasha made the appropriate noises as she quickly changed into close-fitting jeans, soft boots and a cool cotton shirt. She would need a hat, but the one she had brought with her was a straw affair with a scarlet ribbon—hardly suitable to wear with the present outfit.

'Golly, that was quick! You look real neat in jeans,' Cherry approved. 'Mom never wore them. She always wore silky dresses. She and Pop used to have rows about it, because she never tried to fit in with life on the ranch ...'

Cherry was only innocently repeating conversation heard between her parents, but nevertheless Natasha felt guilty about not stopping her, all too conscious that if Jay were to overhear them he would probably accuse her of deliberately snooping on what he would no doubt consider to be private family matters.

'Oh, all grown-ups quarrel from time to time,' she said in response.

'Not like Mom and Pop. They were going to get a divorce. I heard Mom saying so.'

This time it was Rosalie speaking, her blue eyes shadowed by painful memories.

Natasha felt her heart go out to her. No doubt her parents had not even known that their quarrels were overheard, but they had left their mark on both the twins, Natasha saw now.

'Mom said that she didn't love him any more. She loved...'

A small warning sound from Rosalie stopped Cherry from going on. So they did have some awareness that some things could not be talked about, Natasha recognised, as Cherry finished uncertainly, 'Someone else.'

'Have you ever been in love with anyone, Natasha?'

Cherry's question caught her off guard. She paused with her hand on the sitting-room door, and debated about how best to answer the question. In the end, the simplest way was with the truth.

'No, no, I haven't,' she admitted. 'There was a boy when my parents were alive, but I was only fourteen at the time... and after the farm was sold...'

'A farm! Did you once live on a farm? Uncle Jay said that you lived in London and that you wouldn't know the first thing about ranch life...'

'Well, I don't,' Natasha agreed, curtailing the anger spreading through her. Of course, Jay would have tried to poison the girls against her... That would be *just* like him! She was finding it hard to reconcile the bitter, sardonic man who had made no secret of his dislike and resentment of her, with the grandson Tip had raved about during their many conversations. And she was finding it even harder to understand why Tip had seen fit to hand over half of his grandson's inheritance to a stranger, especially when he had appeared to consider Jay such a paragon.

As she remembered it, the only fault Tip had been able to find with his grandson had been his lack of a wife and children... sons.

'The farm my parents had was tiny compared with this place.'

'Tell us about it,' Cherry demanded, slipping her hand into Natasha's as they headed for the stairs.

On her other side, Rosalie took her other hand.

How on earth could she describe to children, used only to Texas, the greenness of her parents' Cheshire farm? It would be impossible, so she temporised by promising to send home for some photographs to show them.

There were boxes of them in her flat, and the old lady who had the flat beneath her, and who had kindly agreed to pop in once a week and check that all was in order, would not mind parcelling up a couple of her albums and sending them off.

Her flat... She gnawed at her bottom lip, suddenly reminded that if she was going to be here for six months, she would have to do something about it. She couldn't leave it standing empty, or rely on Mrs Oates for such a long period of time.

As they reached the bottom of the stairs, through the open front door, Natasha saw a vehicle disappearing in a swirl of dust.

'That will be Uncle Jay taking Mr Goldstein back to Dallas,' Cherry remarked.

And that was another thing. If she was to stay here, she would need some form of transport. A wicked gleam suddenly lit her eyes, a way of getting back at Jay and confirming all his erroneous impressions of her, making her grin a little to herself. So he wanted to think she was a fortune-hunter, did he? Well, let him! He wanted pain? He could have it. And how!

Dolores materialised just as they were about to go out, her expression changing slightly as she saw Natasha's jean-clad figure.

'The girls are just taking me out to see their ponies,' she told the housekeeper. Holding her eyes, she continued calmly, 'You'll know that I'll be staying here for the next six months, Dolores. You must tell me if there is any way I can make myself useful to you during that time.'

She could almost feel Dolores summing her up, and suspected that her offer of help was the last thing the housekeeper had expected.

'We get a mite short of help in the kitchen when Jay entertains out-of-state buyers. How good are you at washing dishes?'

Controlling her temper—she knew when she was being deliberately goaded—Natasha said evenly, '*Very* good. It was the first chore my mother ever taught me...'

'Oh, Dolores, quit teasing her,' Cherry interrupted. 'You know we've got dishwashers to do that.'

Natasha had known it as well. One quick glance round the enormous kitchen, when she had taken her breakfast things into it earlier, had shown her that it was well equipped with everything any cook could desire.

'Um ... well, it's gonna take some acclimatising before that skin of yours gits used to our Texas sun. If you'll take my advice you'll git yourself a hat before you go out in it ...'

Miraculously, Dolores seemed to be softening towards her, although Natasha couldn't understand why.

Dolores herself wasn't so sure either, she only knew that she had looked into those dark golden eyes and received the distinct impression that their owner would find it very hard to lie. She said as much to her husband Miguel later, adding complainingly that the girl must have bewitched her, because everyone knew what she had done to Jay and how she had stolen his inheritance away from him.

The twins' ponies, along with half a dozen or so other mounts, were stabled in their own quarters not far away from the house.

The flat, dust-baked yard and the stables round it were curiously English in design, and for a moment as she stared around her, Natasha felt tears blurring her eyes. Only then did she recognise the enormous strain she had been under since her arrival in Texas.

The yard and its stables were probably Spanish in conception, like the house itself, she realised. She wondered about the history of the house and the family. Tip had told her much of it, but from a blatantly male point of view, mentioning nothing of the women who had lived and loved here.

'These are our ponies,' Rosalie told her, leading her towards two adjacent stalls.

Two pretty cream noses appeared over the top of the half-doors, two pairs of intelligent brown eyes studying the visitors.

Almost from nowhere, a small, bow-legged, grizzled man arrived. He was chewing something which he spat out as he approached them, and Natasha realised it was probably tobacco.

'Well, now...and where have you two imps of Satan appeared from?'

It was strange to hear that faintly Irish brogue mangled by the long, flat vowels of Texas, and it took Natasha a few seconds to recognise the brogue for what it was.

'We've come to see our ponies, and to show them to Natasha, Rory.'

A quick, narrowed glance at Natasha informed her that Rory already knew all there was to know about her, but she refused to let her eyes slide away or her head drop.

'Just come out from England, so they tell me. You'll have to mind that Celtic skin of yours,' he warned her. 'You'll need a hat...'

'I know. I intended to buy myself one in Dallas, but there wasn't time...'

'Boss is going into the city tomorrow morning. I guess he'll give you a ride.'

'Oh, yes, Natasha, and we can go with you. We both need new clothes, don't we, Rosalie? And especially new outfits for Jamie Claire's party next month. We wanted to go shopping with Uncle Jay, but he always gets so impatient.' Cherry made a face.

There were certain things she needed, things she hadn't bothered to buy at home, because then she had anticipated having an overnight stay in Dallas, with some time for shopping. And, besides, there was that matter of her own transport.

'We'll have to see,' she temporised, 'if your uncle is going to Dallas... I thought you two came out here to ride,' she reminded them.

'Ride yourself, do you?' Rory asked her, as she stood carefully to one side, watching as both girls mounted up.

'I used to... as a child. But it's years since I last did.'

'Once you learn, it's something you never forget. We've got a nice little lady's mount at the other end of the yard. Jay bought it for...' He broke off, his ruddy face colouring darkly, as though he had been on the edge of committing an indiscretion.

Natasha deliberately ignored it. After all, it was no concern of hers who Jay might or might not have bought the animal for.

'She hasn't been ridden in a long time. I take her out myself when I get the chance... so she's a mite frisky. Want to take a look at her?'

The girls were leaving the stable yard, and she paused to watch them go.

'Will they be all right on their own?'

'Oh, they'll be fine! A sensible pair they are. They know better than to break any of the ranch rules.

Beyond the yard stretched mile after mile of dusty red earth, all of it empty of any sign of human or animal occupation. In the distance Natasha could just about make out the sight of the huge oil derricks they had flown over last night, now shimmering in the afternoon heat.

'Where are the cattle?' she asked Rory, as she followed him down the yard.

'Well, the breeding stock is kept in special pens and yards. The rest—the beef cattle—they're out on the range. We move 'em closer to the river at this time of year...'

'I understand that Jay's hoping to develop a new breed of beef cattle—with leaner meat...'

Rory's eyebrows lifted in surprise at her interest and knowledge.

'Yep, that's right. Costing him a mite of sleepless nights and money to do it as well... First time he tried, the calves were too big for the cows, and half of 'em aborted. Now he's introduced another strain. Should start calving any time now. We're all keeping our fingers crossed...'

'Only just calving now? They're late, aren't they?'

He looked at her again, and she explained hastily, 'My father was a farmer, in Cheshire.' A faint, nostalgic smile lit her features. 'Calving time was always a very anxious period. Most of them went into labour late at night, especially those that were having problems... My mother used to get up to join him...'

Her smile faded abruptly as she recalled her parents' death and her own subsequent loss, and Rory, sensitive to her pain, didn't press her with any questions.

'Mare's down here,' he told her awkwardly. 'Fine animal she is, although like I said, a mite temperamental. Tip was always on at Jay to get rid of her. At least, he was until he came back from London. Then he seemed to sing a different tune. Here she is.'

The mare was pure bred Arab, with flared nostrils and a satiny coat. She moved restlessly round her stable, rolling her eyes as they approached. Instinctively Natasha held out her hand to her, letting the mare accustom herself to her scent, crooning soft words to her... generations of farming and diluted Cossack blood showing her exactly how to treat the nervous animal watching her so intently.

'Well, now. Raisa has sure taken a fancy to you,' Rory pronounced when the mare regally allowed Natasha to stroke her silky neck. 'Fancy riding her? I could get her saddled up for you...'

'Not today.' Natasha thanked him with a smile. 'As you said, I need to get myself a hat...'

Already she could feel the effect the sun was having on her bare head. A faint feeling of nausea crept through her stomach, and she knew that it was time she got out of the sun. But the girls were still out, and the deep vein of responsibility that her father had passed on to her wouldn't allow her to go in until she knew that they were safely back.

She looked around the yard, searching for a patch of shadow, but there wasn't one. A film of sweat broke out over her skin. Whichever way she turned the sun continued to torment her. She licked dry lips and closed her eyes, feeling the heat beat down on her closed eyelids. This wretched fair skin of hers. Had she had a couple of weeks' holiday she might have stood a chance, but coming straight from the cold dampness of a London summer to the heat and dryness of Texas had made her doubly vulnerable to the overpowering strength of the hot sun.

She blinked a couple of times and then smiled reassuringly at Rory when she saw the concern with which he was watching her.

'Why don't you come and sit down in one of the empty stalls? Get out of this sun. It can be a mite overpowering if you're not used to it. I mind when I first came over from Ireland... Working in Virginia I was then, as a stable lad. Fair knocked me out at times it did.'

He was talking to her in the same soothing voice he used to his horses, Natasha recognised, as she docilely followed him across the yard and into the welcome coolness of one of the stalls. She was out of the sun now, but she suspected that the damage had already been done.

Not for the first time in her life, she cursed her vulnerability to it. She would have been all right if she had worn something on her head, but she had simply not realised it would be so intensely hot.

She sat down on the small stool Rory passed to her, and when he asked awkwardly if she would be all right, she assured him that she was fine.

'I'd better go and get on with my chores, then. I don't want the boss to come back and find me slacking.'

'No,' Natasha agreed. 'He doesn't strike me as the lenient sort.'

The criticism was out before she could stop it, and she saw from the faint frown on the Irishman's face that he didn't like her criticising his employer.

'Oh, he can be hard enough when he needs to be, but he's a fair man...a very fair man. Which is more than you can say for most... He's well liked around these parts and with good reason. Pays good wages, and sees to it that all his staff are properly covered for medical insurance. I had nearly a month off this time last year on full pay.'

Somehow Natasha managed to placate him, although she had to admit to herself, when she was alone, that she found it hard to recognise the sarcastic, contemptuous man who had accused her of being his grandfather's mistress in the almost benign employer Rory rhapsodised over.

By the time the girls returned, her head was throbbing unmercifully; every time she moved, waves of heat and cold washed over her, and her stomach churned nauseously. She had experienced these symptoms often enough before to know that she was in a full-blown attack of heat-stroke.

There was nothing she could do about it. It would just have to be endured. And it was her own fault, after all, but who could have imagined that less than half an hour standing in the sun would be enough to bring on such unpleasant symptoms?

She went out to greet them as she heard the clatter of their ponies' hooves, trying desperately to remain in what little shadow there was as she waited for them to dismount.

She was pleased to see that they had been taught the proper care of their mounts, and that they made sure their ponies were comfortable before handing them over to Rory.

They were just about to return to the house when Rosalie called out, 'Look, here's Uncle Jay...'

Sure enough, as Natasha turned round reluctantly, she saw Jay striding towards them, his boots kicking up small flurries of red dust.

He took off his Stetson as he reached them, wiping a muscular forearm across his face.

'Hot one today, Rory...'

Natasha watched as the girls hung back, obviously longing to run up to him, but just as obviously fearful of doing so. Was this why Tip had made that extraordinary will? Because of the girls? Somehow it seemed out of character. He had scarcely mentioned them to her when he was in London, and yet his conversation had been peppered with comments about his longing for a great-grandson. No, she didn't think that could be the reason behind it...

'Uncle Jay, Natasha needs a hat to protect her head from the sun,' Cherry announced when he at last deigned to notice them.

'And we need dresses for Jamie's party,' Rosalie added. 'Can you take us to Dallas for the day tomorrow?'

'Not tomorrow, but maybe the day after...'

Natasha could see the impetuous words springing to both girls' lips, but they suppressed them, turning disappointed faces in her direction.

'Never mind, tomorrow you can show me some more of the ranch,' she consoled them.

Now that Jay was in the stable yard with them, the atmosphere there had suddenly become very oppressive. Natasha walked past him as delicately as a highly strung mare avoiding a snake, but she had forgotten about the power of the sun, just as strong now as it had been when they first came out. It hit her full in the face, dazzling and then dizzying her, so that she swayed and then cried out as pain exploded inside her head.

She was dimly conscious of pitching forward into painful darkness, of voices, high and tense with concern and fright, and then the comfort of something hard and warm protecting her, blocking out the fierce power of the too-strong sun.

In her confused, half-conscious state, her mind played tricks on her, sweeping back time. She was a little girl again, fainting from heat-stroke in one of her father's fields, when she had disobeyed her mother and taken off her sun-hat.

The sense of strength and protection in the arms that held her now was the same as then, and without needing to give the matter any thought she clung to the body that warmed her own.

She was conscious of movement, of doors opening and then the blessed coolness of air-conditioning. She heard fresh voices, low and composed, and an answering rumble from the chest against which her head rested, without being able to make out what was being said.

She was being placed on something soft and cool. She longed to simply sink back into it, and yet at the same time she fought against losing contact with the man who held her.

Hard fingers prised hers away from the shirt into which they were curled; an even harder profile blotted out the light; a harsh voice calling her back from the past and its comforting memories.

'It's OK, you can stop the play-acting now. You don't have any audience. What are you trying to do? Make everyone feel sorry for you, the way Gramps did? Well, it won't work with me, honey girl. I'm not an old man, vulnerable and lonely...'

His words jerked her back to reality, her fingers releasing their grip of him as though the contact with him burned her, her eyes flying open, what little colour there was in her face leaving it.

It was galling enough to have practically fainted right into his arms, without him now trying to accuse her of having manufactured the whole thing. Just what sort of woman did he think she was?

She already knew the answer to that question, and it wasn't an answer she liked.

Anger came to her rescue, driving the lethargy and nausea from her body, giving her strength to sit up and face him, despite the continued pounding in her head.

'If you honestly believe that about me...that I deliberately tried to seduce your grandfather...that we were lovers...then you don't know much about women...'

'But you're only too willing to be my teacher, is that it, honey?' He stood up abruptly, his mouth hard with dislike and contempt. 'Forget it. Other men's leavings have no appeal for me...'

Natasha almost choked on her fury at his chauvinistic response. How dared he suggest that she had deliberately been trying to make him notice her as a woman? She watched him walk to her door and open it, wishing now, when it was too late, that she had died rather than let him pick her up. How could she explain that it was her memories of her father, her vulnerability to them that had made her forget for a moment who he was and know only that the strength of his body offered her a particular kind of comfort she had not known in a very long time? Her instinctive reaction to being held in his arms had been completely innocent—as free from any sexual undertones as his own attitude towards her, but she would never be able to make him believe it. Never!

But then, why should she want to? Why should she care what he thought about her? Why should she concern herself with his psychological problems—and he obviously had them. He *had* to have to jump to such ridiculously inaccurate judgements about her.

A misogynist, Tip had apparently called him. Was he? Was his antipathy not just for her but for her entire sex? And if so, why?

A brief rap on her door distracted her from her thoughts. Dolores came in, carrying a glass of milk and some sandwiches.

'Jay said you weren't feeling too good, and probably wouldn't be down for supper.'

'Heat-stroke,' Natasha told her wryly. 'Completely my own fault. I went out without a hat. Somehow my one and only straw didn't seem quite the right thing to wear with jeans. I intended to get myself a Stetson while I was in Dallas. I had planned to stay there overnight; I wasn't expecting to be picked up by Jay. In fact, there are a whole lot of things I wasn't expecting,' she added under her breath, but Dolores caught the remark and looked curiously at her.

'Are you trying to tell me you knew nothing about Tip's will?'

'I'm not trying to tell you anything at all, but as it happens, I didn't. I barely knew him, after all, and certainly not well enough to expect anything like that. He didn't even tell me about the twins. All he could talk about was Jay and the fact that he wasn't married. To me, he seemed to be obsessed by a desire for Jay to produce a son or, even better, several sons.'

'That was Tip all right,' Dolores agreed, her manner relaxing slightly as she put down the tray and sat down on the edge of Natasha's bed. 'Well, there's no reason why I should, but I'm inclined to believe you mean what you say. But if that's the case...'

'Why am I staying, instead of simply handing Jay's inheritance back to him? I'm not sure. As I said, I only knew Tip for a week, but he struck me as a very shrewd man, a man who would always put himself and his family first. To leave me so much seems out of character, and yet he must have had a reason for it... If I stay I might find out what that reason was...'

'Mmm...' Dolores was giving her an odd look, something that combined amusement and approval, almost as though somehow she had just passed a secret test.

'The twins tell me that you used to live on a farm.'

'Yes, yes, I did... In Cheshire. It had been in my father's family for generations, but when my parents were killed it had to be sold. I've promised to send home for my photograph albums so that I can show them what it was like. It's impossible to describe to them. Everything was so green.'

There was a wistfulness in her voice that didn't go unnoticed by the older woman.

'Yes, I've heard tell that England is... Jay's brother married an English girl. It wasn't what Tip wanted for him. He'd got something else arranged for him. A girl he'd picked out himself for him, but then Nat went and married this English girl he met in Vegas—a showgirl she was. Tip never approved of her. He and Nat quarrelled badly about it. Tip all but threw him out. It was Jay who persuaded Tip to let him come back. I think Tip might have gotten used to her if the twins had been boys. He was that kind of man,' she added, when she saw Natasha's faint *moue* of distress. 'Yeah, Jay did his brother a real good turn there, but it all backfired in his face and cost Jay dear...' She suddenly seemed to remember exactly who Natasha was, and stood up, reverting to her earlier curt manner, as she indicated the milk and sandwiches.

'Don't worry about the tray, I'll send someone up to fetch it later.'

All in all it had been a very odd sort of day, Natasha thought sleepily less than an hour later, as the sedatives she had taken for her headache began to take effect. Now that she had made the decision to stay here she would have to write to her bank and arrange to have some funds transferred over here. She would need to ... She fell asleep half-way through the thought, dreaming wildly confused dreams in which Jay Travers featured rather disturbingly.

CHAPTER FIVE

'Wake up, Natasha! Have you forgotten that Uncle Jay's taking us to Dallas today?'

Natasha had! She stifled a faint groan as one of the twins tugged on her duvet cover. Opening her eyes, she recognised Cherry. A morning in bed following her brief spell of sunstroke had soon returned her to her normal good health, but for a moment she had a cowardly impulse to claim that she really didn't feel well enough to make the trip into the city.

She squashed it firmly, feeling both cowardly and guilty. The girls were both looking forward to the treat so much that she could hardly explain to them that her own lack-lustre behaviour sprang from her reluctance to spend any more time than strictly essential in the company of their uncle.

In fact, if it wasn't for the fact that she was convinced that there was far more to Tip's will than initially met the eye, she would have been safely at home already. But Tip had obviously wanted her to stay at the ranch. He had *known* that money would never tempt her—after all, she had enough of her own—but his grandson, it seemed, lacked the older man's keen perception.

Scowling horribly, she threw back the quilt and stood up.

'Come on,' Cherry urged. 'Dolores is making pancakes. You won't want to miss them...'

Dolores was a marvellous cook, but the thought of pancakes for breakfast was not one that tempted Natasha's appetitie. What did tempt her, though, was the thought of Dolores's wonderful coffee.

'Give me ten minutes,' she told Cherry, adding reluctantly, 'What time are we supposed to be leaving?'

'Straight after breakfast. Uncle Jay did tell us last night,' Cherry told her in a faintly aggrieved accent. 'After you'd gone to bed...'

Natasha bit her lip. Every night since her arrival at the ranch, she had discovered some excuse for going to bed early so that she could avoid spending any more time than strictly necessary in Jay's company. It wasn't that she was frightened of him— far from it, despite that brooding, almost menacing quality she sensed about him at times. No, her desire to hold him at a safe distance sprang as much from emotional vulnerability as physical dread. But why on earth should she feel like that? What possible emotional risk could Jay be to her?

She didn't know; she didn't *want* to know, she admitted restlessly as Cherry disappeared, and she opened her wardrobe doors to look for something to wear.

A day in the city...shopping...lunch... She mentally reviewed the pretty, colourful wardrobe she had bought especially for this trip, and then rejected everything in it, in favour of an outfit she had bought in the spring from Harrods.

The tailored navy skirt flattered her slender hips; the navy and white blouse, with its puffed half-sleeves and neat little collar, adding a touch of demure femininity. Over the top went an unlined seven-eighths-length coat in navy with chalk-white lines making bold checks. In all, it was an elegant, even sophisticated outfit. The sort of outfit worn by a confident woman; the kind of outfit that would show Jay Travers the type of adversary he had to deal with.

Dolores frowned at her when she walked into the breakfast-room, dourly indicating the jug of coffee she was putting down.

'It's fresh, so don't let it go cold.'

Already Dolores had discovered one of her weaknesses, Natasha realised as she helped herself to the fragrant brew.

A careful but thorough inspection of the breakfast-room had assured her that Jay wasn't in it. Both girls had heaped plates of pancakes, and although Natasha's stomach heaved a little as she watched Cherry ladling thick syrup on to hers, it settled down again quickly enough.

'Uncle Jay says we're to be ready and out front by ten,' Rosalie informed Natasha.

'Pa always used to get furious with Mom when she kept him waiting, do you remember, Cherry?'

Sadness shadowed Rosalie's face as she spoke, and Natasha felt an instant surge of sympathy. She knew what it was like to lose dearly loved parents. She felt her throat thicken with tears—not for herself, but for the girls. Jay, with his dour, almost bitter remoteness, was surely not the right man to have charge of these two young people with their specific emotional needs. They needed someone they could relate to, someone who would listen to them, who knew what they were going through...

Someone like herself, perhaps. Hence Tip's will?

And yet the older man had not struck her as the type who would have sufficient sensitivity to think of the girls' emotional needs.

'They were always fighting,' Cherry's voice was bleak and curt, and as she looked up at her in startled surprise, for the first time, Natasha saw something of her sardonic uncle in the young girl's face.

Rosalie made a small *moue* of distress, but Cherry wouldn't be silenced.

'You know they were. I reckon they would have got a divorce. Mom was always going on about how she had never really loved Pa, how she hadn't wanted to marry him and go live on a ranch, and how he had persuaded her... Sometimes I used to think she preferred Uncle Jay to Pa.'

There was a small silence and then Dolores bustled in, commanding that they finish their pancakes. Had the housekeeper overheard what Cherry was saying, or was her appearance merely fortuitous?

Had Jay secretly been in love with his brother's wife? Was that what made him so withdrawn and cynical? Was that why he had never married despite his grandfather's wish that he should?

It made unpleasant sense. Natasha gnawed at her bottom lip. How dreadful it must have been for the girls' father if it was true! How dreadful for all of them. Was that what had made Jay hate the female sex—an unwanted desire for his brother's wife? And he *was* the type who would put loyalty to his brother before his own feelings, who would even blame the woman who was the innocent cause of those feelings.

She was spending far too much time worrying herself about Jay's motives, she told herself as she finished her second cup of coffee and got up.

There was just enough time for her to go back upstairs and freshen her make-up before they were due to meet Jay at the front of the house.

Upstairs in her room, she thanked her lucky stars that she didn't need to wear very much on her skin. The humidity and heat of Texas were not conducive to retaining a perfectly made-up skin. Hers was good enough to withstand exposure with just a light covering of sun screen and a touch of creme blusher to highlight cheek and browbones.

A soft slick of glossy lipstick added another touch of colour and she was ready.

Her shiny straw hat with a wide brim that framed her face would protect her from the sun, and as an added precaution she picked up her sunglasses. She wasn't going to fall into the same trap twice and be accused of faking her *malaise* simply to get Jay's attention.

That accusation still stung; all the more so because it was not true, and because she had always loathed those sort of feminine wiles. She hated the role Tip seemed to have cast for her. Playing a *femme fatale* had never held any appeal for her, and it was that aspect of her role that she disliked the most—more so in some ways than being accused of being a gold-digger—perhaps because this latter accusation would be so easy to disprove, should she ever wish to do so.

She deliberately timed her arrival downstairs to coincide with that of the twins. Like her, they were dressed for the city, although casually in attractive cotton bermudas, with matching patterned tops.

'Jenneth bought these for us, the last time we went to Dallas.'

'Jenneth was Uncle Jay's girlfriend once,' Cherry confided pulling a face. 'We don't like her very much. She's too bossy. We're both glad that she married someone else, aren't we, Ros?'

'Yes,' her twin agreed. 'But sometimes I think that she would still rather have Uncle Jay than Howie. Gramps used to say that when she was around Jay needed protecting from himself. It was because of Gramps that they didn't get married. She had no money, and Gramps said that she was just after Jay's, didn't he, Cherry?'

All too conscious that she should have stopped this conversation long before it had reached this stage, Natasha still experienced a guilty desire to learn a little more about this unsuspected aspect of Jay's personality. Had she been wrong then in thinking he loved the girls' mother? It seemed so... And she could certainly see Tip refusing to allow his grandson to marry badly. And yet, what she had seen so far of Jay had not inclined her to the view that he would be easy to dictate to. Far from it, in fact. Of course, Tip had held the purse-strings...

She sighed faintly, her thoughts shooting off at so many tangents that she couldn't control them.

'Jenneth and Howie are coming over to dinner tomorrow night,' Cherry told her. 'Howie's in oil, and he's really, really rich. Much richer than Gramps or Jay...'

'Yeah, and doesn't Jenneth just love letting us all know it?' Rosalie commented in a drawl that was astoundingly like her uncle's.

Both girls giggled. 'Wait until you see her, Natasha! Silk dresses and loads and loads of jewellery...'

'And make-up...lots and lots of that, too. And the way she looks at Uncle Jay...'

'Yeah, I wonder who's going to protect him from himself now that Gramps has gone?' Rosalie asked a little mournfully. 'I'd hate for Jenneth to divorce Howie and come and live here. She'd send us both off to boarding school in Europe, I just know it. She doesn't like us.'

'Yeah, Gramps used to say she was like a pie that was all crust and no meat,' Cherry confided, 'and that if Uncle Jay took a bite it would choke in his craw!'

It was *definitely* time to put an end to these confidences and, taking hold of both girls, Natasha said firmly, 'That's enough, both of you. I'm sure your uncle would be far from pleased if he could hear what you're saying about his private life.'

Fortunately, before either of them could make a rejoinder, Jay himself drove up in the same vehicle he had used to transport them from the airstrip on Natasha's arrival.

Now, as then, Natasha elected to sit in the back with the girls. This time, she looked around with interest as they drove out to the airstrip, and Natasha noticed two distinctive and different breeds of cattle grazing on either side of the tarmac road.

An expertise that she had forgotten she possessed informed her that these were the two breeds

Jay was hoping to cross to get a new, hardier strain of animal.

When she said as much Jay was so surprised that he turned his head to look at her, almost releasing his hold on the steering wheel.

'You've been busy doing your homework,' he said airily when he had recovered from his shock. 'But those tactics won't work on me, so you're wasting your time.'

Natasha felt her skin burn, and would have made an equally offensive response, if she hadn't suddenly remembered that they weren't alone.

Luckily, they were almost at the airstrip and in the bustle of getting out of the truck and into the plane, the girls forgot what they had overheard.

It didn't take long to get to Dallas. Natasha's feelings were still stinging from Jay's sarcasm, and she refused the hand he held out to her as she got off the plane, turning her face aside, so that the wind whipped against her skin, and she had to reach up to clutch on to her hat.

In her high heels, she teetered dangerously on the steel steps. She heard Jay curse, and then his arms came round her, blotting out everything else, the harsh male scent of him surrounding her, invoking a weak, feminine dizziness that was her body's instinctive response to his masculinity.

He released her almost immediately; the whole incident had only lasted seconds, and yet it was imprinted on her memory and her senses in a way that was having a devastating effect on her.

She felt boneless and oddly shaky, torn between a need to cling to him and a need to push him away; shocked by her reactions and yet, at the same time, strangely exhilarated, as though she had discovered a magical elixir of which only she knew the source.

Dallas was hot, and very windy. To Natasha's surprise, a sleek chauffeur-driven limousine was waiting for them. Jay shepherded all three of them into it, and then, to her consternation, climbed into the back seat himself to sit next to her.

The pressure of his lean, hard thigh against her own was shockingly disturbing, and even though she knew it was not done deliberately she was intensely conscious of every tiny movement of his body as Jay leaned forward to instruct the driver.

'I've organised a room for you at the Hotel Crescent Court. We'll go there now, and then the car and the driver will be at your disposal for the rest of the day.'

Natasha wanted to protest, but the words stuck in her throat. This wasn't the way she was used to shopping, ferried around in air-conditioned luxury in a chauffeur-driven car, but Dallas wasn't London, and she was aware from Tip's conversation that Americans never walked when they could ride. From the girls' lack of reaction to Jay's statement, it seemed as though shopping with the luxury of a chauffeur-driven car was nothing out of the ordinary to them, and so Natasha kept her own thoughts very firmly to herself.

The hotel and its surroundings took Natasha's breath away, and she stared out of the car window as the girls pointed out the triple towers that housed the complex's office blocks, and the tri-level landscaped shops and galleries.

Even in a city where money was virtually no object, this complex of hotels, office space and shopping malls must surely stand out, Natasha thought, awed, as the car slid to a silent halt outside the hotel entrance.

With a brief word to their driver, Jay escorted them all inside. In the close confines of the car it had seemed only natural that she should be so intensely aware of him, but now that they were out of the car it was still there and she didn't like it.

Unlike many of the other men in the hotel lobby, who were wearing casual clothes, including jeans, Jay was dressed in an immaculate pale grey fine wool suit. He ought to have looked uncomfortable in it, given his ranching life, but he didn't. Even his pale grey Stetson didn't look entirely out of place. If she was honest with herself, she would have to admit that it gave him a certain hard-edged, very masculine air, emphasising the intensely male aura that seemed to surround him.

She wasn't the only one to notice it, Natasha reflected wryly, noticing the way the striking, attractive blonde behind the reception desk started to glow with animation as Jay walked towards her.

From their soft-voiced exchange, it was obvious that the girl knew Jay's name. There was a subtle blend of respect and curiosity in her voice that Natasha recognised as female responsiveness to Jay as a man, as well as a more worldly recognition of his financial status.

'Here you are.'

Jay handed Natasha a room key.

'The room's yours for the day. I'll meet you here at one o'clock for lunch—Jake knows to get you back here for then. We'll be leaving at five. That should give you enough time to get all you want.'

He started to move away and then hesitated, frowning as he reached into the inside pocket of his suit, and withdrew an envelope which he handed to her.

Natasha shivered sensitively as their fingers touched. It was as though an electrical impulse shot through her. She watched the way his dark eyebrows contracted, almost meeting over the jutting bridge of his nose.

'There should be enough there to cover all the girls want. If there isn't, tell the store to charge it and send the account to me. You shouldn't have any problems.'

A brief glance in the envelope made Natasha's eyes widen even further. She didn't know what prices were going to be like in Dallas, but to get through that little lot the girls would have to be dressed from head to foot in designer outfits, not once, but several times over.

Before he left, Jay pointed out to her where she could find the hotel's coffee shop. On seeing the anxious, although patient, expressions in the twins' eyes, she said firmly that she didn't need anything and that they might as well start shopping right away.

Their first port of call was one of the new malls in the Crescent complex.

Almost straight away they found a pleasant boutique stocking pre-teenager clothes, and although privately Natasha thought that silk shorts and tops were ridiculously fussy and impractical for girls the twins' age, she did like the fresh, bright cottons that the assistant brought out to show them.

Tactfully directing the girls' attention away from those things she thought too old, or too impractical for them, she helped them both to choose a pair of pedal-pushers each, with patterned cuffs, and matching tops. There were pretty flat-soled shoes to go with them, and although the outfits weren't cheap, the quality of them was good.

A stroll along the walkways revealed other boutiques, all with mouth-watering window displays, and jewellers shops that made Natasha blink in astonishment. The only purchase she made for herself was a soft cream Stetson and a couple of pairs of slim-fitting jeans, from a small store set out like a saloon bar from a television western.

Although the hat made her feel acutely self-conscious, she recognised that she would need it if she was to accompany the girls on their rides round the ranch. As yet she had explored nothing of her new environment, and if she was to stay here for six months . . .

A small frown gathered on her smooth forehead. Initially, when she had made that impulsive decision, she had been fired by temper and righteousness; now in the cold light of reality she wondered if she had the strength of will to carry it through. Although Dolores had softened slightly towards her, she knew that if it came to a show-down the Mexican woman would align herself very firmly on Jay's side.

Jay could, and most likely would, make life extremely difficult for her. She gnawed at her bottom lip; she could think of at least half a dozen excellent reasons for leaving Texas, and only one good one for staying, and that was her conviction that

Tip had made that will for a specific purpose, and that for her to leave would be letting him down.

Perhaps it was the very fact that he seemed to have chosen to put all his faith in her rather than his grandson that made her feel she ought to stay. The vulnerability of such an action reached out to her, touching her own inner sensitivity.

Rosalie, tugging at her arm, brought Natasha out of her reverie. 'Just look at that car—it's really neat. Just what I want when I get my licence.'

They were standing outside a car showroom window and, like the twins, Natasha gazed admiringly at the sleek lines of the Mercedes sports car. Oddly enough she had once contemplated buying such a car for herself, but had rejected the idea on the grounds that it was totally impractical for use in a city such as London. Now as she gazed at the shiny new vehicle a tiny demon of mischief stirred inside her, and she remembered her idea of getting herself a car to shock Jay. She needed a car while she was out here in Texas, and if she bought one like this it would mean she had made a commitment to staying that she could not go back on. A car like that would give any woman confidence—panache. She stared thoughtfully at its shiny red paintwork, and wondered a little dazedly why she was hesitating. After all, it was not as though she couldn't afford it. Hitherto she had been thrifty with her inheritance, barely even spending the interest it accumulated. She made a few swift mental calculations: a telephone call to her bank in London . . . a few moments explaining the position to the sales staff.

'Let's go inside,' she said to the twins. 'I think I might buy it.'

Somewhere at the back of her mind lurked the pleasant thought of the shock with which Jay would receive her purchase. He would be bound to suspect then that she wasn't the penniless fortune-hunter he seemed to think. He would be forced to back down, to swallow his insufferable accusations. She swallowed hard . . . perhaps he might even apologise to her . . .

She took advantage of the girls' momentary shock to sweep them inside.

The salesman listened as she carefully explained her situation to him, the girls enthusiastically roaming around the showroom.

A telephone was put at her disposal while she telephoned London. Her bank, although a little surprised by her request, promised to immediately telex the funds to her.

A brief test drive, during which she found that she loved the easy way the car handled, confirmed her rash decision.

With a promise that the car would be delivered to the ranch within a couple of days, Natasha took her leave of the salesman.

All the way back to the hotel, the girls chattered enthusiastically about the car.

'Gee, won't Uncle Jay be surprised!' Cherry exclaimed. 'I can't wait for them to deliver it. Will you take us both for a ride?'

Telling them that she would, Natasha shepherded them to where their chauffeur waited with the car.

In a slow drawl he informed her that it was time they returned to the hotel for lunch. They arrived back with half an hour to spare. Just enough time to go up to their room and have a wash and brush up before lunch.

The room was enormous by British standards; the bathroom vast and equipped with a wide range of toiletries.

Natasha elected to have a quick shower, re-dressing and then renewing her light make-up while the girls had theirs.

Feeling much fresher, she accompanied them back down to the elegant dining-room.

Nearly all the women diners were dressed el-egantly, some of them even wearing hats; and a good many of them seemed to be lunching in all-female groups of fours or sixes.

'Their husbands will be having lunch at the Cattleman's Club,' Cherry whispered in response to Natasha's comment.

'Look, here's Uncle Jay...'

The moment Jay joined them in the lounge, a waitress appeared to take their order for pre-lunch drinks.

Like the girls, Natasha opted for a long, cool, fruit concoction. Jay ordered whisky and water.

'Well, kids, did you get what you wanted?'

His smile... his relaxed air of amiability were di-rected at the twins and deliberately seemed to ex-clude her, Natasha noticed.

'Yeah, we got some great things, but wait until you see what Natasha bought, Uncle Jay!'

A cool, derisive look slanted her way.

She had known, of course, that the girls wouldn't waste much time in telling him of her surprise pur-chase, but for some reason a deep sense of unease gathered coldly in the pit of her stomach. As Cherry burst into excited speech, describing the splendours of the car, and how they had just walked into the showroom and bought it there and then, Natasha's feelings underwent an about-turn, and she longed to hold back the girls' excited chatter.

Was she the only one to notice how cold and condemning Jay's face was growing? Was she the only one of the small group to be aware of the quality of the silence gradually descending on them? Couldn't the twins see how furious their uncle was?

To Natasha's relief, the *maitre d'* came to escort them to their table before the twins noticed anything lacking in their uncle's response.

Over a very pleasant meal of fresh scallops followed by steak and a mixed salad, Natasha felt her tension grow and grow, to the point where she could barely eat a mouthful of food. Something had gone badly wrong. Far from being put properly in his place by the knowledge that she could afford to purchase such an expensive toy, Jay seemed to be regarding her with even more distaste and bitterness than he had done before.

Lunch wasn't a protracted affair, and Jay had to leave immediately afterwards to attend some further business meetings.

Natasha and the girls spent their afternoon doing some more shopping. Natasha was tempted by a silk dress she saw in a boutique window and, egged on by the girls, went in to try it on.

As she had ruefully suspected when she first looked at it, it might have been made for her. With a wry shrug, she decided 'in for a penny in for a pound', and recklessly agreed to buy it.

FREE-GIFT COMPUTER CARD

TEAR OFF HERE AND MAIL THIS CARD TODAY!

H A R L E Q U I N F R E E G I F T D E P T.

MAIL THIS FREE-GIFT COMPUTER CARD
to receive 4 FREE Harlequin Presents... PLUS a FREE Surprise Bonus!

Use this heart to get a
FREE SURPRISE BONUS!

FREE!
AFFIX THIS
STICKER IN
SPACE AT
RIGHT

Yes! Send me 4 Free Harlequin Presents plus A Free Surprise Bonus. Then, send me eight new Harlequin Presents each month and bill me just $1.99 per book (26¢ less than retail). No postage and handling charges. If I am not fully satisfied, I may return a shipment and cancel at any time. The 4 Free Books and Free Surprise Bonus remain mine to keep.

108 CIH CANK

□ MR.
□ MRS.
□ MISS

FIRST NAME   INITIAL   LAST NAME

PRINT YOUR NAME HERE FOR DATA PROCESSING (Please PRINT in ink)

ADDRESS   APT.

CITY   STATE   ZIP

Offer limited to one per household and not valid for current Presents® subscribers. Prices subject to change.

FREE GIFT DEADLINE:

A	U	G	U	S	T	3	0	1	9	8	8

TEAR OFF HERE AND MAIL THIS CARD TODAY!

Printed in U.S.A.

DATA PROCESSING ☛13-48
0000000000000000000000
45 46 47 48 49 50 51 52 53 54 55 56
1111111111111111111111
2222222222222222222222

PLACE
GOLD HEART
HERE

to receive
your
FREE
Surprise
Bonus

NO POSTAGE
NECESSARY
IF MAILED
IN THE
UNITED STATES

APPROVED
FREE-GIFT OFFER

BUSINESS REPLY CARD
FIRST CLASS   PERMIT NO. 717   BUFFALO, NY

POSTAGE WILL BE PAID BY ADDRESSEE

 Harlequin Reader Service ®

901 Fuhrmann Blvd.,
P.O. Box 1867
Buffalo, NY 14240-9952

The dress was by a British designer, in a style often favoured by the Princess of Wales, with a dropped waistline, and a ruched band of fabric over the hips—a style that could only be worn by the slim-hipped. The silk was white, with an all-over pattern of small black splodges, and here and there a flower outline traced out in buttercup-yellow and orangey red—not the sort of thing she normally chose, but for all its demure round neckline and long sleeves it was undeniably the sort of dress a woman wore for a man. Perhaps it was something to do with the softness of the silk, or maybe it was that tantalising slit up one side—Natasha didn't know. She already had a good black linen jacket she could wear over it if need be and a pair of black and white court shoes so, firmly resisting the girls' entreaties to buy something else, she shepherded them out of the shop.

By the time they had paused mid-afternoon to have coffee and ice-cream, and completed the rest of the girls' shopping requirements, it was time to head back to the hotel.

'I'm bushed,' Cherry commented, stifling a yawn as their limousine dropped them outside. 'I don't know how on earth you can walk all day in those heels, Natasha.'

'I'm used to it,' was Natasha's response.

Working in the exclusive Bond Street gallery had meant that she always had to be smartly dressed, and that included wearing high heels. She was also used to walking on hard pavements, unlike the girls, and when she said this they looked at her, puzzled for several seconds, until she realised why, and amended with a smile, 'I mean sidewalks. We call them pavements at home.'

From then on until they reached their room, Natasha kept them entertained by explaining the origins of the English language, telling them how it could be traced back to the influences of various civilisations.

'I never knew English could be so interesting,' was Rosalie's comment as they walked into their room.

The first thing Natasha did was to slip off her shoes, and wriggle her toes.

'Umm...bliss! What time is your uncle due to get back?'

'Not for a while yet. I'm hungry,' Cherry complained.

'Well, we could order something from room service, if you like.'

'No.' Cherry shook her head. 'I'd like to go down and have something in the coffee lounge, then we can sit and watch everyone come and go.'

In the end all three of them went down, Natasha simply ordering coffee for herself and then sitting back as she watched the twins devouring their sandwiches with healthy appetites.

'There's Uncle Jay!' Rosalie suddenly commented, putting down her milk shake.

'Yuck, and just look who he's got with him,' Cherry agreed in a disgusted voice. 'That's her,' she told Natasha, as the latter glanced over in the direction of Jay and his tall, ethereally blonde companion.

'You know, the one we were telling you about, who Jay was going to marry. I bet she knew he was coming to Dallas and tracked him down.'

An odd feeling engulfed her as Natasha watched Jay with the other woman. She said something to him, touched his sleeve with pretty deference, gazing up at him, her mouth trembling slightly.

They were too far away for Natasha to see Jay's expression, but there was something about the tender, caring way he bent towards the other woman that made her acutely conscious of a vast emptiness in her own life that could have been filled by a man who loved her and whom she loved in return.

The lack of a husband and children, which she had never previously regretted, now caused a deep ache in the region of her heart. She looked at the twins and then she looked at Jay, and she was overwhelmed by a sense of loss so intense that it almost brought tears to her eyes.

What was happening to her? Why on earth was she going all emotional, simply because she saw Jay looking at another woman with tenderness and concern? She must be going soft, losing her grip.

'I hate her. And I wish she'd leave Uncle Jay alone.' The harshness in Rosalie's voice brought her out of her own disturbing thoughts.

Against her will, her attention was drawn once again to the couple who stood so close together, Jay's dark head bent so comfortingly towards the blonde one of his companion. He touched her hand, gently, reassuringly, and a wave of intense aching swept through Natasha. How long had it been since she had been able to lean on someone, the way Jay was being leant on now? How long had it been since someone had cared enough about her to want to protect her?

'Mom hated her, too,' Cherry added thoughtfully. 'I wish we could think of a way to make her leave Uncle Jay alone.' Her eyes lit up and she turned enthusiastically towards Natasha. 'Perhaps you could pretend that Uncle Jay was in love with you.'

Oh, for the unbounded scope of a child's imagination, Natasha thought ruefully, her own having difficulty in adapting to this unlikely scenario.

'Uncle Jay's seen us,' Rosalie hissed. 'He's coming over...'

As Natasha watched discreetly, she saw him detach himself from his companion, and walk over to them with his cattleman's easy lope.

'Shopping all done, kids?'

'You bet! It's all upstairs in our rooms.'

'Well, I think we'd better get up there and collect it, and then head out for the ranch.'

He accompanied them up in the lift, and Natasha was appalled by the sensation of claustrophobic awareness of him that the ride aroused.

With both girls standing between them, it was ridiculous that she should be so aware of him, and yet she was. When the girls bounded out of the lift ahead of them, she felt so tongue-tied that she couldn't have spoken even if she had wanted to.

The feeling of loneliness, of betrayal almost, that she had experienced when she saw him standing with someone else had left her so confused and frightened that she was barely capable of forming a coherent thought.

Alongside that pain ran another, almost as bewildering. She wanted him to like her, to approve of her, to smile at her as he had at that other woman. But why? He was everything she most disliked: self-opinionated, chauvinistic, uncompromisingly determined to stick to his own views, right or wrong, judgemental, and worse. And yet, here she was, quivering like a weak-kneed idiot and aching for him to turn and smile at her with genuine liking.

Almost in a daze she followed the girls into their room, standing by while they gathered up packages, which they loaded into Jay's waiting arms.

'These are yours, Natasha,' Cherry reminded her, handing her her own parcels.

Out of the corner of her eye she saw Jay's frown, and her heart dropped. She longed to scream at him that what she had bought she had paid for from her own money, but pride wouldn't let her. He was subjecting her to that same derisively cold smile he had given her earlier when the twins had told him about her new car. Was he resentful of the fact that *she*, a woman, could afford such a vehicle? Was that the problem?

Loaded up with parcels, the girls left the room. Shakily, Natasha made to follow them, but Jay grasped her arm ungently, kicking the door closed with one foot.

'Not yet, you don't,' he grated, swinging her round to face him, and tumbling the packages on to the large bed. 'I want to have a word with you. What the hell do you mean by buying yourself that car? What did you do—charge it to the ranch? Well, I've got news for you . . . if you think that Gramps's

will entitles you to go round spending money like
it's going out of style, you've got one hell of a shock
coming to you!'

Anger, pain, shock—all of them were there. All
of them intense and agonising, so much so she was
hard put to know which she felt the most.

'What are you going to do about it?' Her throat
arched, her head tilting back so that she could look
into his face; so that her eyes could meet his and
he could read the scorn and fury burning there.
'Rescind the sale?'

Her nails dug into the palms of her hands as she
prayed that he would; her earlier feelings of loneliness and longing forgotten. Oh, God, if only he
would. She'd love to see the look on his face when
the salesman told him just how that car had been
paid for. Did he honestly think she could go out
and buy herself an expensive piece of machinery
like that without so much as a by your leave? Did
he really have such a low opinion of her that he
thought her capable of such cupidity, such greed?

'Why don't you just go right ahead?' she challenged him through gritted teeth.

'And make myself and my grandfather a laughing
stock throughout Texas? No way... You've played
it smartly right enough, honey. You get to keep your
car, but nothing in life comes free, and you'll have
to pay for it one way or another.'

'Who's going to make me?' Natasha challenged,
her Russian temper suddenly blazing out of control,
as she looked at him, ashen-faced and gold-eyed.
'You?'

She saw an instant too late that she had pushed
him too far. She felt the edge of the bed behind her

as the hardness of his body pushed up against hers, propelling her backwards, his arms tightening, imprisoning her, as he said harshly, 'You're damn right, I am.'

And then his mouth came down on hers, punishing, ravishing, assaulting her senses and her defences in a way that left both bruised and defiled.

It was a kiss without passion or mercy, a cold, hateful domination of her body, that revealed her essential feminine weakness. She knew that if he chose to rape her here and now there was nothing she could do about it, and she also knew that he was well aware of her fear and vulnerability.

As he released her and stood slightly back from her, nothing could stop her from brushing shaking fingers across her mouth, in a childish and instinctive attempt to wipe away the taint of him.

Something flickered in his eyes, some deep instinct she recognised and rejected in one choking, agonised breath. She knew that he was going to kiss her again, and yet she didn't move—*couldn't* move, simply standing there like a mechanical toy.

'No woman brushes the taste of me off her mouth as though she's tasted poison, especially a woman like you!'

She heard the anger throbbing in his voice and winced beneath the bite of his fingers as they clamped round her upper arms.

His breath grazed her skin, clean and fresh, oddly disturbing to her senses.

His head bent again, and when she tried to evade the punishment she knew was coming, quickly averting her head, his hand captured it, sliding into her hair, arching her throat back under the pressure his fingers were exerting, his voice thick and raw as he said softly, 'If you hate my touch that much, perhaps this is the best punishment of all.'

She cringed beneath the slow movement of his mouth along the exposed column of her throat, expecting with every second to feel the sharp bite of his teeth inflicting pain, bunching her muscles against him until she was shaking with tension.

Quite when her feeling of fear was eclipsed by the slow-growing dawn of fevered excitement, she didn't quite know. One moment it seemed she was resisting him, fighting him with every locked muscle; the next her body was turning traitor on her, her skin quivering beneath the slow assault of his mouth. A feeling of languor stole over her, a weakness that made her boneless and compliant, eager for the taste of his mouth when it eventually reached hers.

Mindlessly she clung to him, unaware of anything other than the fact that this man had unlocked doors within her that she hadn't even known existed.

His mouth taught, teased, explored and finally swept them both to a fury of passion that rendered them equally vulnerable to the sensations racking them.

Natasha came to her senses first, alerted initially by the hot touch of his hand against her breast, and secondly by the sound of the girls' voices outside in the corridor.

When she pushed him away, Jay stood tautly watching her with eyes that didn't focus properly, his skin flushed with the same heat burning inside her.

For the first time in her life she had known the fierce lure of a man's passion, and she was still half drugged by it.

'Damn you!' Jay muttered savagely. 'Damn you to hell, you little...' He said a word that cut into her like a knife. 'Don't be misled by this! The men of my family seem to have a weakness for women of your type, but in my case it's a weakness I don't intend giving in to.'

Before she could object, before she could tell him how wrong he was about her, the girls burst in, demanding to know what had delayed them.

Natasha turned her back toward them, and gained a certain amount of savage satisfaction in leaving Jay to deal with their questions.

CHAPTER SIX

THE car which Natasha had bought with such pleasure stood reproachfully and unused in the garage Jay had grimly allocated to it.

It wasn't just pride that kept Natasha from telling him the truth and explaining that she had bought the car from her own money—after all, ultimately, he must surely realise the truth when no invoice was forthcoming?

No, there was more to it than that. Something much, much more... Something insidious and dangerous that gnawed at her and made her feel more vulnerable than she had ever felt in her life. She needed the barrier of reminding herself how irrationally and unfairly he had behaved towards her; how he had misjudged and abused her. She needed it and she was determined to retain it.

Even so, no matter how justifiable her actions and her right to spend her own money as she chose, she found it impossible to touch the car.

The girls had both begged for rides in it, suggesting that she take them on a visit to see their friends, but always she found some excuse to put them off.

Instead, she persuaded them to take her riding round the ranch. Rory had saddled the mare for her and, although at first the girls had been inclined to tease her for the way she rode, it had only taken Rory's comment that the English way of riding was the only correct way, to silence their teasing comments.

Her new Stetson protected her from the sun, and soon she was able to appreciate how vast an area the ranch covered.

She had deliberately stayed out of the way the evening after their return, when Jenneth and her husband had come over to dinner, not wanting to watch Jay dancing attendance on the other woman, giving to her the kindness and courtesy that was so lacking in his manner towards herself. She was not eager to examine too closely her motives behind this reaction; she only knew that the intensity of her sexual reaction to him left her feeling acutely vulnerable and frightened.

Even then, when surely any man of sense must have realised how innocent and untutored she was, he had gone on blaming and accusing, she reflected acidly, as she slid tiredly off her mount's back.

Today she had spent almost four full hours in the saddle, and her muscles were starting to ache a little.

She had been surprised and pleased at the ease with which her old riding skills had come back to her. Once when they were out, the twins had pointed out Jay and some of his men to her, but although Jay had looked in their direction he had not ridden over to them.

Tonight Jenneth and her husband were coming to dinner again. The twins had given her the news dolefully, convinced that the blonde was making a play for their uncle.

'You wait and see. She'll get a Mexican divorce from Howie, and she and Uncle Jay will be married before he's had time to turn round.'

'Would that really be so bad?' she had asked, painfully aware of her own sharp thrill of anguish.

'Yes! She'd pack us off to Europe as soon as she could. Why can't you get Uncle Jay to fall in love with you, Natasha? We'd much rather he married you...'

Rosalie, always more intuitive then her twin, must have read something in her face, because she shushed Cherry, and said awkwardly, 'You don't have to do that, but if you could just pretend that he was in love with you, that would frighten her off.'

'Yes, I read this story once, and that's just what happened,' Cherry piped up, relating an improbable scenario with relish, apparently unaware of the fact that one word from Jay would make nonsense of any attempt on Natasha's part to pretend that they were in love.

The twins' concern for their uncle wasn't entirely selfish, Natasha knew. They both cared very deeply for him. They were also frightened and vulnerable: frightened that if he did marry Jenneth they would lose him, and she could understand that fear all too well...

According to the twins, Jay and Jenneth had quarrelled and broken off their long-term romance, Jenneth departing in high dudgeon to Fort Worth, returning as the wife of Howie.

Now, it seemed, she was tired of that marriage, and Jay was tired of being without her.

Every time she pictured Jay and the blonde standing together, a strange sensation of pain and loss permeated her, a sensation that persisted no matter what she did to banish it.

She had spent so much time since her arrival avoiding him that it had become second nature. Thus it was something of a shock to walk into the main hallway of the ranch house, just at the very moment he was coming out of his den.

For a moment it seemed as though they were both held in some strange thrall, staring at one another in tense silence.

It was Jay who broke it, his voice harshly bitter, as his glance flicked her trim, jean-clad figure. 'You've not been out in your new acquisition yet, I see. What are you trying to do? Impress me with your sense of remorse?'

The unfairness of it infuriated her. Her eyes, always the first indication of her changing mood, burned bright amber, flecked with gold, the colour leaving her skin abruptly as it always did when she was angry.

'Impress *you*!' she said scornfully. 'I'd have to be crawling in the gutter before I'd want to do that, and even then I'd think twice.'

She felt his immediate response in the hot blaze of his eyes, his body so tautly controlled that she could almost feel the tension in his muscles. As she almost ran past him she felt his anger beat against her; knew that he ached to take hold of her and slowly deprive her of breath, of life, and yet she didn't regret her words. She had thrown them down between them like a gauntlet, wanting him to experience the furious impotence that overwhelmed her each time he misjudged and insulted her.

Now she had done it, and when the madness boiling her blood receded she would probably regret her folly. But right now, it was a pleasure to turn at the top of the stairs and look down to where he stood watching her, dark colour burning his cheekbones like two angry weals, the bones standing out in sharp relief beneath his tanned skin, his eyes glittering with dark rage.

Never had she been more aware of his Indian ancestry; it showed in the taut angularity of his bones, in the tension of his muscles, in the complete stillness of his body as he willed it to a state of control.

Civilisation had been stripped away to reveal the savage, just as when her temper was aroused she reverted back to the blood she had inherited from her Russian ancestress.

It came to her with a start that it was a bond they both shared: alien and dangerous blood mixed volatily into their more phlegmatic inheritance.

She didn't want to go down for dinner, but she had run out of excuses. If she stayed upstairs tonight Jay would think she was cowering there out of fear.

She dressed quickly, almost angrily, her movements lacking their normal feminine elegance. One after the other she discarded outfits, not really knowing what she was looking for until she found at the back of the cupboard an outfit she had bought in Harvey Nichols on impulse just before she left.

It was a two-piece designed by Flora Kung, a golden-yellow silk skirt, short and tapered, falling from a neat waistline. The jacket was a wild mixture of golden-yellow, white and cerise, with long sleeves and a wrap-over bodice that fastened with tiny fabric-covered loops and buttons on a wide, fitted waistband.

Every time she moved, the silk clung and whispered seductively. The golden yellow colour enhanced her rich hair, her eyes still glowed fiercely topaz, her skin flushed delicately and becomingly. Almost as though she were donning special armour, she was wearing the silk underwear she had bought on an extravagant impulse. Silk stockings clung to her legs, and her backless sandals were golden-yellow leather, with orchid leaves over the toes.

A dusting of golden powder and bronze eyeshadow, an application of mascara and lip gloss, a spray of the Giorgio perfume Adam had bought her for Christmas applied to her pulse points and she felt every inch the voluptuous *femme fatale* Jay seemed to think she was.

She met the twins just as they emerged from their rooms. Both of them stared at her in gratifying fashion, but she didn't realise why until Cherry hugged her enthusiastically and whispered, 'Great! You're going to do it, I knew you would. You'll have no problem convincing Jenneth that Uncle Jay's in love with you, dressed like that.'

Natasha stared at her. In her fury at Jay, she had completely forgotten the girls' obsession with their uncle's relationship with Jenneth.

She opened her mouth to deny that she had any such intentions and then closed it again as Dolores appeared at the top of the stairs.

'Time you was all down with Jay. His guests will be arriving any moment.'

Her chance was gone, the girls were racing downstairs ahead of her, firmly convinced that she was all set to play the role they had cast for her, and the fault was hers. She shrugged lightly. Well, by the end of the evening they would realise they were wrong. They would be disappointed, of course, but when she explained they would soon understand.

Natasha reached the bottom of the stairs just as the doorbell rang. Jay himself emerged from his den to answer it, and so Natasha was standing almost right beside him when Jenneth and her husband walked in.

The blonde frowned and came to an abrupt halt the moment she saw Natasha, while her husband's eyes widened appreciatively.

'Well, now, Jay! That's some pretty lady you've got here,' he drawled with what Natasha privately considered to be over-fulsome flattery.

Nevertheless, she hid her distaste and extended her hand to shake his, grimly waiting for Jay to denounce her, as the female who had seduced and exploited his grandfather. But to her surprise he said only, 'Natasha is a friend of...of the family's, and she's staying with us for a while.'

Obviously Jenneth knew nothing about his grandfather's odd will. Was it because Jay was frightened that he would lose her a second time if she realised he was not the sole beneficiary?

Natasha wondered grimly. The blonde's rather cold blue eyes narrowed, and she said in a playful voice that held more than an underlying hint of ice, 'Not a friend of *yours*, surely, Jay? At least, not one I've ever known existed...'

To her own amazement, Natasha heard herself saying softly, 'Oh, Jay and I have been friends for a long time. We were introduced by his grandfather...'

Somehow or other her arm had found its way through Jay's and she was clinging to his side, much as the blonde woman had done when Natasha had seen them in Dallas.

One part of her mind refused to accept what she was doing, looking on instead in bemused and horrified bewilderment.

Beneath her fingertips, Jay's arm was as rigid as that of a statue. She heard him breathe in sharply, and out of sheer devilment ran her fingers lightly against his exposed wrist. The sensation of his dark fine hair against her fingertips was oddly stimulating, engrossing her to such an extent that she forgot the reason why she was doing this. She heard Jay expel his breath harshly, and risked a flirtatious look up into his furious eyes.

He might well look furious, she thought bemusedly. So would she in the same circumstances. What on earth was she trying to do, get herself scalped? Because that was what she read in his eyes: a promise of a long and painful death.

She had *had* to do it, or disappoint the twins, she told herself virtuously as she released him and turned to make small talk with Jenneth's husband, judiciously deciding not to go in for overkill. Jay deserved to suffer a little... after what he had done to her...

It stunned her, this capacity and desire for revenge. Where had it come from?

It was too late for second thoughts or fear now, there was no going back. Jenneth was glaring at her with open venom, the twins hovering in the background. Both gave her encouraging grins as she turned her head and saw them. What on earth had she done? She realised that she was shaking, and wondered what had possessed her. She must have been out of her mind!

She comforted herself with the thought that Jay would find some way of reassuring Jenneth that she had only been play-acting, thinking that if he tackled her about it, she could always... Always what? Let him think that she was what he had accused her of being? She shrugged aside the pain slowly seeping into her. Why did she always feel this anxious desire to court his good opinion? Why had she so instantly felt that flash of antipathy and dislike towards Jenneth? Why had it felt so *right* to stand at Jay's side, her hand through his arm, her body lightly touching him?

'That's a rather unusual outfit,' Jenneth commented as they all walked into the dining-room. She was dressed in sugar-almond pink, with flounces, and her implication was quite plain.

Never had Natasha taken so much pleasure in straying from her normal subdued elegance.

'Isn't it?' she agreed with a smile. 'I bought it in Harvey Nichols... where the Princess of Wales shops, you know...'

As she had expected, Jenneth looked slightly discomfited, and Natasha saw no reason to add that as far as she knew Princess Diana had never bought an outfit by the same designer.

'Really?' Jenneth made a slight recovery. 'But then, of course, she's blonde . . . and these are such vivid colours . . . with red hair . . .'

'Yes, redheads are lucky,' Natasha agreed. 'We don't have to stick to insipid pastels . . . Such a relief, especially when one becomes older. There's nothing more ridiculous than a woman dressed in baby pinks and blues once she's past the age for them, don't you agree?'

Another killing glance joined the one Natasha had already received, but, fortunately, before she was called upon to think up any more acid remarks, Dolores came in to announce dinner.

It came as something of a shock to Natasha to discover that she was seated at the opposite end of the table to Jay, almost as though she were the hostess.

As she sat down, Cherry whispered to her in explanation, 'Dolores doesn't like Jenneth, either. She says once Jenneth comes in she's walking out.'

It seemed that she was part of a wholesale conspiracy to rescue Jay from the clutches of his would-be wife! Just how appreciative of this concerted effort he was likely to be she wasn't too sure, but why should she concern herself with Jay's feelings? When had he ever concerned himself with hers?

The meal that followed held all the ingredients of a black farce. Jenneth complained that she couldn't eat the shellfish. At the same time as she was listening to Jay expressing concern, Natasha was wondering if Dolores had deliberately chosen to serve the delicious mussels in their white wine sauce, knowing that Jenneth wouldn't be able to eat them.

The Texan equivalent of a traditional British Sunday roast lunch followed, and again Jenneth merely picked at her food, this time claiming that so many calories would ruin her figure. Since she was slender almost to the point of frailty, Natasha could only see this complaint as a rather obvious means of drawing Jay's attention to her fragile frame.

A quick look at Howie confirmed that he was watching his wife's flirtatious manner towards Jay with frowning suspicion. Telling herself that it was not her job to rescue Jay from the consequences of his folly, Natasha suppressed a sigh as she valiantly engaged the older man in conversation.

Once she had got through his seemingly impenetrable outer shell of toughness, Natasha discovered that he was a surprisingly interesting man: a lover of both ballet and opera, as he shyly confided in her.

Once or twice as they talked, Natasha was conscious of the fact that they were coming under scrutiny from Jay, and he finally interrupted Howie harshly to say, 'Natasha, Jenneth was asking you a question.' Natasha retaliated with a sweet smile and a soft, 'Oh, I'm sorry, darling...' before turning to look at the blonde.

She could almost feel the twins' glee, and certainly Jenneth looked far from pleased at the intimate way she had addressed Jay.

After dinner they all went out on to the porch to have their coffee, at Jenneth's insistence.

Howie grimaced and complained that he would be eaten alive, but Jenneth's girlish pout won the day.

'Jay, you must show me your mother's garden. I always think this is the best time of the year for it... Jay's mother came from Boston, and when she was first married, she had the most beautiful garden designed in the English style. It's watered by a special underground sprinkler system. Have you seen it yet?'

As it happened, Natasha had. The girls had taken her round it, and she had been amazed and awed at the work that must have gone into creating such a very pretty and English garden in such an alien landscape. A box hedge surrounded it, the paved walks enclosed with traditional border plants; there was a rose arbour covered in sweet-smelling damask roses and a clinging wisteria. There was even a herb garden, which Cherry had told her contained some of the plants originally used by their Indian ancestress.

In the evening the garden was an especial delight, its scents released into the night air. Natasha often went for a stroll around it before going to bed, but she suspected it wasn't so much the scents that Jenneth wanted to enjoy as the solitude, and Jay's company.

It was sheer devilment and nothing else that made Natasha reach out and place lightly constraining fingers on Jay's arm, her pout almost matching Jenneth's, as she murmured seductively, 'Oh, darling, please stay here. I've seen so little of you today... I'm sure Jenneth, being such an old friend, will understand. Perhaps she could show Howie the garden, since she's so familiar with it.'

Behind her Natasha just caught the sound of a stifled giggle, one of the twins, no doubt! At her side, she could feel the furious disbelief emanating from Jay, but oddly he didn't say anything.

It was rather touching, that small vein of gentlemanly courtesy; of a code of behaviour now long dead running through the otherwise austere and ruthless harshness of his personality.

Much as he longed to deny the claims she was making on him, Natasha saw that he would not, not in public, at least. But there would be a reckoning to come. However, the presence of the twins made her feel safe, and if need be she could avoid Jay for long enough for his temper to have died down. The twins were quite right, anyway, she decided firmly. Jenneth was not the woman for him. She was too greedy, too grasping. In fact, she was surprised that Jay was deceived by her. How odd men were... leaping to totally erroneous conclusions on the smallest of evidence, and yet unable to see what lay plainly beneath their noses.

Howie was standing up, and Jenneth had no alternative but to go with him. The look she darted Natasha as she stalked past her promised retribution.

Smiling complacently, Natasha sat back in her chair. It was very pleasant here, sitting on the long porch, and enjoying the coolness of the evening breeze.

Her complacency vanished abruptly when, after a whispered conference, both the girls stood up.

'We're going to bed now,' they claimed in unison. 'We're both tired.'

They were gone before Natasha could stop them; leaving her alone in the darkness with Jay.

Even with the width of the wicker table between them, she could feel the searing fury of his anger. She wanted to get up and run, but she didn't think she had the nerve.

'Now,' he said menacingly, the soft, low sound of his voice reaching her through the half-lit darkness making her jump. 'Perhaps you would care to tell me exactly what's going on.'

She didn't even think of lying to him; there was something too threatening and dangerous in the very quality of his stillness for her to do that.

'The twins are frightened that you're going to marry Jenneth. They wanted me to...'

'Warn her off?'

It was too dark for her to make out his expression properly, but the grimness in his voice made her shiver violently, despite the warmth of the evening.

He got up and came slowly towards her, her own chair almost falling and trapping her as she jumped up too quickly, desperate to escape.

'Oh no, you don't!' he rasped, grasping her arms painfully. 'You might have got away with playing those tricks off on other men, but not with me you don't. The way you were coming across all through dinner made it plain just what sort of relationship is supposed to exist between us. No one makes a fool out of me like that without paying for it, lady. Especially a little tramp who's had more men in her bed than she can remember.'

She knew that he was going to kiss her, and instinctively jerked back from him.

'Stop acting like a scared virgin. We both know I can make you want me...'

'No!' Natasha choked out the denial, infuriated by his claim, and yet knowing it held a grain of truth... It was only half a truth though; he wanted her too, no matter how much he might prefer to deny it. Hadn't he already told her as much?

As though her denial, and the way she instinctively arched back in his hands to avoid any contact with his body brought out a latent well of savagery in him, he swore under his breath and dragged her against the hardness of his body.

The sheer bulk of his muscled frame pressing her back against the house wall made her panic. She struggled wildly, hitting out at him with bunched fists, adrenalin pumping fiercely through her veins as she responded to instincts as old as time, in her efforts to escape from his physical domination.

'Stop it! Stop pretending you're scared.'

His words reached her, but meant nothing... She *wasn't* pretending! Why should she? She gave a frantic push that almost unbalanced him and then cried out in shock, the sound smothered against her lips by the hard pressure of his.

I can make you want me, he had claimed, and appallingly it was true. Her senses recognised him, wanted him, she realised as she froze in shock.

He made a sound in his throat, the pressure of his hands slackening, his fingers caressing where they had gripped. His mouth moved hungrily on hers, his tongue pushing fiercely past the barrier of her closed lips. He kissed her almost as though they were already lovers, she realised, and the sounds he was making against her mouth were a mixture of anguish and need. He wanted her... She felt it in the aroused movement of his body against hers.

Her breasts swelled and hardened, aching in a way that was totally unfamiliar. When he slid one hand over the silk of her top to caress her, her body arched instinctively to facilitate his movements.

She wanted him in a way she had never wanted any other man. She shuddered as the knowledge ripped through her.

Someone called Jay's name. It took her several seconds to realise that it was Jenneth, and that the other couple were returning to the veranda. Almost as though it had taken him time to realise what was going on, Jay's reactions were slow too, his movements slightly clumsy as he released her and pushed her away. Even in the darkness she could see the heavy rise and fall of his chest, hear the tortured sound of his breathing.

'Damn you!' he swore at her, wiping his hand across his mouth in much the same gesture that she had previously used to wipe his touch from hers. 'Damn you to hell!'

She fled before the other couple reached them. Let Jay make whatever explanations he chose to the other woman. She no longer cared.

But she did care, Natasha recognised bleakly as she prepared for bed. She cared far too much...far, far too much.

'Uncle Jay's gone to Dallas again. Do you think he's meeting Jenneth?' Cherry scowled horribly as she asked the question.

The twins and Natasha were sitting in Jay's mother's 'English garden'.

'I don't know.'

Jay had paid several visits to Dallas since the débâcle of the dinner party. No one knew what had transpired between Jay and the woman whom the twins suspected was determined to become his wife, after the twins and Natasha had gone upstairs. Perhaps he had told Jenneth the truth: that she, Natasha, had simply been deliberately trying to stir up trouble between them by pretending to a relationship that did not, and never would exist.

'You were great, Natasha. You did your best,' Cherry comforted her. 'But that Jenneth...'

'I wish Uncle Jay really would fall in love with you and marry you,' Rosalie interrupted, speaking almost fiercely. 'And then you would always stay here...'

'I'll be here for six months out of every year,' Natasha told her.

'That's not the same... If you and Uncle Jay were married then you would have babies, and we'd all be a real family...

Natasha didn't know what to say.

'Look, someone's coming,' Cherry announced.

A dust cloud along the straight road through to the ranch house confirmed her claim.

'Let's go and see who it is.'

Unwillingly, Natasha followed the two girls to the front of the house.

Jenneth was just stepping out of an expensive limousine. She was alone, Natasha noticed, sighing over the other woman's elegance. *She* was dressed in jeans and a cotton top, whereas Jenneth was wearing a silk dress and a matching cocktail hat, her blonde hair pleated in a neat chignon.

'I want to talk to Natasha alone,' she announced, dismissing the twins with a regal wave of her hand. 'Let's go somewhere where we can't be overheard, shall we?' she suggested once they had gone.

The only place Natasha could think of was the English garden, and so, reluctantly, she led the way there. She could think of only one thing Jenneth would want to discuss with her. Jay must have told her the truth.

She sat down and waited for Jenneth to begin the attack.

She didn't have to wait long.

'Look, I know exactly what you're doing out here,' Jenneth told her acidly, 'but you're wasting your time. The old man might have hand-picked you to be Jay's wife, but he won't marry you.' Her mouth curled scornfully. 'Oh, you might think you fooled me with that idiotic little bit of by-play the other night, but I know Jay. He's a man with strong passions... very strong passions... You've never shared those passions. Anyone can see that! I suppose that's why Tip picked you.' Her mouth curled bitterly again. 'A virtuous English virgin for his only grandson. That would be typical of him and his dynastic ideas. But Jay won't marry you, no matter how long you hang around...'

She paused to draw breath and Natasha got in quickly and coolly, 'I presume when you say that you must be speaking from personal experience?'

Her dart hit home; a tide of angry colour swept over the other woman's carefully made-up face. 'All

right, so Tip did manage to part us, but he wouldn't
have done it if it hadn't been for that bitch, Helen,
Nat's wife. And believe me, the fact that Jay didn't
marry me won't help you. He's a romantic, you
see, and he's in love with a woman he can never
have.'

She laughed triumphantly as she saw Natasha's
shock. 'Oh, it's true! I'm surprised you haven't
heard all about it. Quite a shock it all caused at the
time. Two brothers both in love with the same
woman. Two brothers—one married to her and one
not. Oh, yes, it's all true. She threw herself at Jay
from the moment she arrived... Well, Nat never
was the man that Jay is... and she soon realised
that, when it came down to it, Jay was the one who
would get the ranch. She almost succeeded as well.
She and Jay were going to run off together.

'She was going to leave here and get a divorce,
and then she and Jay were going to get married.
They had it all arranged, but then Nat found out
and drove after her. He found her in Dallas just
before she reached the border and forced her to
come back with him. They had a fight. No one
knows what really happened, but the car went off
the road and both of them were killed.

'So, you see, Jay will never marry now. His
heart's buried in Helen's grave. Of course, he's still
a very... sensual man. He has his needs, needs that
he can't satisfy with a passionless woman like you.'

'But that he can satisfy with you?' Natasha interrupted quietly. 'You've nothing to fear from me,
Jenneth,' she added in open disgust. 'I wouldn't

lower myself to giving my body to a man who I knew was only using it to forget someone else.'

For the second time she saw ugly colour fill-Jenneth's face. In other circumstances she might have felt sorry for the older woman, but now, now she was too bitterly aware of her own pain, her own vulnerability.

Now so much that had been a mystery was explained. Now she suspected she knew exactly why Tip had made that will. He had known that Jay would never marry of his own volition. He had known that the woman his grandson loved was dead, and so he had brought *her* here, as bait; willing her half of his property so that Jay would... What? Marry her to regain it?

A bubble of mirthless laughter rose in her throat. Tip had made one vital miscalculation. He had forgotten the effect of his macho boasting and embellishment of their innocent relationship. Because he, like Jenneth, had seen instantly that she was sexually inexperienced, he had believed that Jay would see it, too. But Jay hadn't. He only saw her as his grandfather's leavings.

She couldn't stay here now. She would have to leave. She bit her lip as she watched Jenneth stalk away, leaving behind her the venom of her sting, firmly implanted in Natasha's heart. It would hurt to leave the twins. She would feel that she was letting them down, but she had no alternative.

She would forfeit her inheritance, but what did that matter? She had never wanted it in the first place. Never even remotely considered wanting it.

Only now, when she was contemplating the fact that very soon, very, very soon, she would never see Jay again, did she realise how much that would hurt. Perhaps it was as well that she was leaving, while she still could.

CHAPTER SEVEN

'NATASHA, come downstairs! You've got a visitor.'

Cherry burst excitedly into the room where Natasha was sitting, thinking how best to write to her solicitor explaining the position she found herself in, and asking his advice on how she might renounce her unwanted inheritance, and yet preserve some rights towards remaining in contact with the twins.

After a good deal of long and painful thought, she had decided that this was her only course of action. She would have to leave Texas, but somehow she would see to it that she was able to remain in touch with the girls, thus ensuring that they didn't lose complete faith in her.

For a moment her heart sank as she contemplated another venom-loaded interview with Jenneth, but then she realised Cherry's enthusiasm hardly suggested that the other woman was her visitor. But who on earth would visit her out here?

As she followed Cherry downstairs, the girl refused to divulge the name or identity of the unknown caller, simply pushing open the door to the ranch's main drawing-room so that Natasha could go in.

To her shock, standing in front of the huge fireplace was Adam!

The sight of him wearing one of his formal dark Savile Row suits, his eyes a little wary, was so unexpected that she forgot all the reservations she had previously had about him and hurried towards him, greeting him enthusiastically.

'Adam! What brings you here?'

'A client wanted me to accompany some antiques he bought, to make sure they arrived safely. I had some time to spare, so I thought I'd look you up.' His eyes narrowed assessingly. 'It's quite some inheritance Tip left you.'

Instantly Natasha frowned. 'How do you know about that?'

Adam shifted his weight from one foot to the other uncomfortably. 'Oh, I must have heard it somewhere in Dallas. You know how people like to gossip.'

She did, and she also knew Adam—always the man for the main chance. Her mouth compressed a little. She was just about to tell him that he had wasted his time in coming out to see her, when a sudden thought struck her.

Fate had presented her with an ideal excuse for leaving Texas, *and* with her pride intact. She didn't need to write to her solicitor about renouncing her inheritance. She could fly back to London with Adam and do it in person!

In fact . . . hot colour stung her cheeks as she recalled Jenneth's acid comments about Tip's plans for her. How many other people had put the same interpretation on his actions? How long would it be before one of them said something to Jay that would force him to see the truth: namely, that his grandfather had never viewed her in the light of his own bedmate, but as his grandson's wife?

Where initially she had anticipated with relish his discovery of his misjudgement of her, now she dreaded it. The very last thing she wanted now was for Jay to realise how lacking in sexual experience she really was, and to start pitying her for it. No, a little gentle flirtation with Adam as her willing partner was exactly what was needed right now. That way no one would be surprised when she announced she was flying back to London with him. She need not say when she would be coming back...
Quickly her mind sifted through the possibilities, blocking out the scornful little voice that warned her that she was running away.

'How long do you have to stay out here?' Adam asked her. 'There was some mention of a certain amount of time that had to be spent out here to fulfil the terms of the will.'

'Oh, I can go home any time I want to, really,' Natasha told him evasively. 'In fact, I was thinking of making a flying visit quite soon.' No need to tell him too much... 'Perhaps I could go back with you?'

She slipped her arm through his and smiled up at him, hating herself for what she was having to do, but knowing that she must.

When his hand covered hers, hot and moist, she almost shuddered. His flesh felt so soft, so alien, so different from the callused hardness of Jay's hand, she realised, mentally jerking away from the realisation like a frightened filly.

'You know I've always liked you, Natasha. More than liked you... And not just because of the money. Come back with me and let me show you how much.'

It was more, much more than she had hoped for, and yet Natasha experienced a tiny frisson of distaste at the way she had manoeuvred him. It didn't really help much, either, to remind herself that her main interest for him was her wealth. She hated using people. She always had but, if she stayed, how long would it be before Jay lost his temper with her again...before he touched her again, kissed her again? Her whole body burned violently. She closed her eyes, trying to blot out the memory of his mouth against hers, but the ensuing darkness only reinforced her tormenting mental images. He affected her as no man had ever affected her. She *wanted* him to touch her, to kiss her. She wanted that and she despised herself for it. She was too vulnerable to him.

'We could have something good between us, Natasha.'

She felt Adam's lips move against her hair, and immediately drew back. At the same time the door opened and the twins came in, both of them giving her accusing looks.

What on earth had she done? She introduced them to Adam, whom they treated with wary politeness. What had happened to their earlier enthusiasm?

Throughout the rest of the afternoon, the twins didn't leave them alone for a moment, giving her scant chance to make any real arrangements to leave.

She knew where he was staying in Dallas, and she would just have to telephone him there, she decided, on a faint sigh.

'I really ought to be leaving. I have a dinner engagement this evening...'

He glanced at his watch, and made a fussy gesture adjusting the cuff of his jacket. It was an irritating habit of his which she had noticed before, and which she felt sure would grow even more irritating were one forced to live with it day after day.

She went with him to his hire car, submitting to his dry kiss, keenly aware that the twins were observing them from the veranda.

'I'll give you a ring tomorrow,' she suggested. 'When exactly do you fly back?'

'I'm not quite sure yet, but instead of ringing why don't you come to Dallas? We could have lunch together.'

Over lunch they would have enough privacy for her to discuss her plans for leaving—she didn't want the twins to overhear them until she was ready to tell them her decision herself.

She was a little late going downstairs for dinner, and found that the twins and Jay were already seated when she walked into the dining-room.

Dolores, who had relaxed considerably towards her, fixed her with a curt frown as she slipped into her chair, and in fact the whole atmosphere inside the room was decidedly cool.

'The girls tell me that you had a visitor this afternoon,' Jay commented, once Dolores had served them.

Natasha blinked a little at the coldness of his tone.

'Yes. My...an old friend,' she amended, realising that it might be dangerous to her plans if she described Adam as her ex-employer.

'He wants Natasha to go back to London with him,' Cherry announced, stunning Natasha to silence. How much of their conversation had the girls overheard—and how? Had they actually been eavesdropping? She frowned at both of them and received a flushed and defiant look from Rosalie in return.

'He was talking about Natasha's money, too, wasn't he, Rosalie? The money that Gramps left her...'

Now it was Natasha's turn to colour brightly. How on earth could she correct the totally erroneous impression the twins' innocent chatter was giving Jay? Any explanation could only make things worse.

She risked a glance at him and saw that there was a white line of temper round his mouth, and that his eyes were glittering dangerously.

Her appetite suddenly fled. She pushed away her plate and stood up. 'I'm sorry... I'm not hungry tonight. If you'll all excuse me...'

She was running away and she knew it, but she simply didn't have the strength to face Jay right now.

She was sitting by her sitting-room window staring into space when the door suddenly burst open.

'Still here, then?' he snarled at her. 'Not run off to join your lover yet? Did the pair of you plan it all right from the start? Is that how it was, Natasha? *Is it*?' He shook her, making her feel so dizzy that when he abruptly released her, she had to cling to the chair for support.

'I don't know what you're talking about,' she told him huskily.

He stared at her for a moment, eyes narrowed, skin stretched tight across his cheekbones.

'What I'm *talking* about,' he enunciated with soft savagery, 'is you and your ... boyfriend, setting up a nice little trap for my grandfather, with you as the very tempting bait. He took that bait, didn't he, Natasha? And he was so besotted with you that he left you half of this place. But you got more than you bargained for, didn't you? You got responsibility for the twins thrown in with all that money, and a will that ties you down to spending six months out of every year here. What does he say to that? Does he know that if you leave here you forfeit everything?'

It was on the tip of her tongue to tell him how wrong he was, and that she was more than happy to give up everything Tip had left her, apart from her guardianship of the girls. Instead, she suppressed her denial and taunted softly, 'What makes you think we're leaving? Adam and I could get married and live here. That way I won't have to give up a thing, will I?'

She had never known before that she was such a good actress. Jay was livid. She could see it in the furious clenching and unclenching of his hands.

'You bitch,' he said hoarsely at last. 'You little bitch ... and you'd do it too, wouldn't you? But I'm not going to let you.'

He was coming towards her, menacing her with every step he took, and her adrenalin-fuelled courage fled, leaving in its place shock at what she had done, and fear of the retribution it would bring.

It was too late to back down now, all she could do was to say defiantly, 'You can't stop me. I can marry who I want. There was nothing in the will that says I can't!'

His lips curled back from his teeth in a dangerous smile. 'So it's marriage you want, is it? Well then, it's marriage you shall have. But not to your pretty blond-haired lover, not to a man who's going to take away what rightly belongs to me!'

Real fear hit her now, constricting her stomach, and making her cry out protestingly, 'No, Jay, I won't marry him. I . . .'

'It's no good. It's too late. You've made me see how vulnerable I am. No, the only way to make sure this ranch is safe . . . the only way to stop you from squandering and destroying it, is to marry you myself!'

It was the very last thing she had expected to hear. She stared at him, the colour leaving her skin, her eyes darkening with shock.

'Marry *you*? No . . . No . . . I can't!'

He smiled again, but there was no mirth in it, no warmth.

'You can't do it, Jay. You can't make me!'

It was true, surely. He couldn't make her, and yet there was something so sure and so determined in the way he was looking at her, that she suddenly felt that there was nothing he could not accomplish if he wished to.

Panic hit her. She started to babble nervously, telling him that she would renounce her share of their joint inheritance, that she would go away and never, ever come back, but he just kept on looking at her with that same calculating, cold look.

'You say that now, but how long would it take you to change your mind? The moment you got out of my sight, you'd be hiring some fancy lawyer to claim that you'd rescinded your share under duress. No… Marriage is the only answer.' He said it almost to himself, almost as though she wasn't there.

'You can't! You don't love me.'

Now he did look at her. His eyes widening, a frown furrowing his forehead as he looked at her as though he'd never seen her before.

'Love?' He said the word as though it came from an alien language. 'My God, you dare to say that to me?' He reached her in three strides, taking hold of her, and staring down at her. 'You, who have given your body to God knows how many men for greed and possibly worse… Love! Love doesn't exist… I thought I had it once, but it was just a chimera, just an illusion… a mirage created by another greedy woman, who wanted this place, more than she wanted me.'

'You mean the twins' mother?' she blurted out before she could stop herself.

He released her as though her skin was acid.

'Who told you about her?'

'Jenneth… Jenneth told me that you loved her…'

His mouth turned downwards. 'So *Jenneth* told you, did she?'

For some reason he looked bitterly amused.

'You can't marry me, Jay,' she protested as positively as she could, hating the way her stomach muscles quivered. What was happening to her? Why did he have the power to have this devastating effect on her?

'I can and will,' he contradicted her flatly. 'Some folks around here are even going to expect it—darling.'

Too late she remembered how she had flirted with him during the dinner party, and bit down hard on her bottom lip.

It was ridiculous to feel this fluttering sensation of panic tinged with pain. After all, he couldn't *force* her to marry him.

Someone knocked on her door and pushed it open.

'Phone for you, Jay,' Dolores announced. 'It's the Cattlemen's Association. Said it was important.'

If Dolores was aware of the tension crackling between the two of them she didn't show it.

She and Jay left together. The housekeeper hadn't exhibited the smallest degree of curiosity or surprise at finding Jay in her room, Natasha realised. In fact, there had even been a certain degree of acceptance in her briefly appraising glance at them. Almost as though she was measuring them together as a couple.

The thought disturbed her. All the more so because she could not automatically reject it as being impossible. It was just as well that she had made arrangements to see Adam tomorrow! The sooner she was home in England the better. The air out here must be affecting her common sense, she decided uneasily. She felt so jittery and tense. The warm, masculine scent of Jay's body still lingered in her nostrils, and she was as acutely aware of him as though he was actually in the room with her.

Ten o'clock. Too early to go to bed, and yet the evening stretched emptily ahead of her. She wanted to deny the effect that Jay was having on her, but honesty would not let her. Her nerves felt as though they had been scraped raw. This constant battling with Jay, and trying to keep at bay her own physical vulnerability to him, were taking their toll on her.

The tension invading her body refused to be quelled. She was wound up so tightly that she couldn't bear to sit down. How on earth was she going to sleep? Her glance fell on the tray of drinks. They had been there ever since her arrival. Normally she never touched alcohol, having discovered in her late teens that she had no head for it.

Her doctor, when she had once complained of this to him, had smiled a little and explained that there were those people for whom one glass of wine could have nearly as much effect as others experienced after an entire bottle.

Over the years she had come to accept that half a glass of wine was as much as her system could tolerate, but tonight... She looked at the tray again and noticed the bottle of brandy. One small glass of that, and nothing would keep her awake. She thought about the broken nights, tormented by disturbing dreams, and succumbed. She needed the restorative effect of a proper night's sleep, and tonight, she decided grimly, she would have it.

She went over to the tray and looked for a brandy glass, but found only a large whisky tumbler.

Not being a spirits drinker, she had no idea how much to pour, but the small amount in the bottom of the glass made her frown and add a more generous measure. After all, what did it matter if she did get a little tipsy? She was going straight to bed.

She would drink this now. Have a bath, and then if she didn't feel sleepy she would pour herself another small measure.

The alcohol stung her throat and warmed her stomach. Almost immediately she could feel its effect on her tense body. The muscles at the back of her neck ached painfully, and she massaged them with one hand, only half aware of the insidious effect of the alcohol as it sped through her body.

She had just decided that perhaps one small glass wasn't going to be enough and poured herself a second when the bedroom door opened.

'We didn't finish our conversation,' Jay told her abruptly, coming in.

'Only as far as you're concerned,' Natasha said recklessly. 'I have nothing I want to say to you.'

He was looking at her half-empty glass and frowning. 'Have you been drinking?'

His obvious disapproval made her defiant. Tossing her head she said sharply, 'Is there a law that says I can't?'

Wilfully she walked back to the cabinet and poured herself another measure, turning to face him as she drank it.

She knew instantly that she had made a mistake. The alcohol went to her head immediately. The room started to sway and she concentrated desperately, trying to banish the cloudiness attacking her brain.

Her faintness retreated, an unfamiliar sense of well-being taking its place. She felt strong enough to take on the entire world, never mind Jay Travers!

'Please leave my room,' she demanded, testing her new-found courage and delighting in the strength of it. It was true that her words sounded rather slurred and odd, but plainly Jay made sense of them because anger was taking the place of his frown as he said irately,

'Not yet, we have to talk.'

'What about?' Natasha taunted light-heartedly. 'Our marriage?'

She was stunned. What on earth had made her bring that subject up?

'Don't push me too far,' Jay warned her.

'Why not?' To her own amazement she heard herself giggling. 'What are you likely to do? Carry me off and marry me out of hand?'

Through her giggles she heard his harsh, in-drawn breath. 'That might not be a bad idea,' he told her savagely. 'In fact...'

He was coming towards her. Something danger-ous gleamed in his eyes. She knew she ought to move, to run, but somehow she couldn't make the effort. He was going to kiss her, she could sense it. Did he know how vulnerable she was to that par-ticular form of persuasion?

Just for a second she struggled against the com-pelling sensation of his mouth moving against her own as he imprisoned her within the hard barrier of his arms, and then her defiance melted beneath the slow surge of heat encompassing her. Dimly, a warning bell rang, telling her that she was being foolish, that she was not in control of either herself or the situation; but she ignored it, clinging mind-lessly instead to the strength of Jay's body.

His mouth tormented her, teasing and promising. He was whispering something against her mouth and she strained to catch the words.

'Marry me,' he demanded softly. 'Come away with me tonight and marry me, Natasha.'

He was touching her, stroking her skin in such a way that she couldn't think straight. She felt muddled and confused. Her body ached to be closer to his, but her mind warned her that she was heading into danger. What was he trying to do to her?

'We couldn't get married just like that,' she protested, trying to fight against the insidious tug of her senses, and to free her brain from the effects of the brandy. He was confusing her with the gentleness of his voice and touch.

'Why not? My plane's on the airstrip. We could fly over the border into Mexico and be married by morning.'

Married! She felt the tiny thrill that ran through her veins, and before she had time to react to it he was kissing her again, bemusing her with the desire he was arousing within her. She swayed closer to him, unable to hide her feelings.

As warm darkness closed in around her she thought she heard Jay make an odd sound of triumph deep in his throat, but it was gone before she could analyse it, and he was lifting her, carrying her out of her room and into the darkness of the Texan night.

And that was the last thing she remembered properly until the small plane started to descend through the darkness.

Hazy images of being carried through the house and driven to the airstrip floated through her mind, but even now she still felt woozy, the effects of the alcohol still powerful enough to bemuse and cloud her brain.

The scents of the Mexican night, the taxi ride through the small town; these were blurred details she was vaguely aware of as she occasionally lifted her head from its comfortable resting place against Jay's shoulder. His arm was round her, holding her close to him. It all felt so deliciously right. She snuggled deeper into his side, burrowing against him, making a small sound of pleasure like a purring kitten.

He looked down at her briefly. She felt so fragile, so vulnerable . . . and she was still knocked out with alcohol. His conscience pricked him but he silenced it. She did not deserve either his compassion or his consideration. Fate had seen fit to present him with this opportunity and he would be a fool not to take it. He smiled grimly to himself, imagining what her reaction was likely to be when she realised what had happened, and then turned his attention to the taxi driver, giving him directions in fluent Mexican.

Once, long ago, he had assisted a friend with the arrangements for a romantic run-away marriage. He hadn't known then how useful he would find what he had learned on that occasion.

CHAPTER EIGHT

NATASHA was in a church. In a small, plain church standing in front of a priest who said familiar words to her, in an unfamiliar accent. She recognised the words, and responded to them automatically, shocked to suddenly feel herself held and kissed.

She looked up with dazed eyes at the man holding her.

'Jay...'

He smiled at her, but his smile wasn't right.

'Yes, Mrs Travers?'

Something was wrong. That wasn't *her* name. She was so confused. She put her hand to her head, and started to stumble. Jay said something to the priest in a language she couldn't understand.

She had to sign something. Her name...the letters wavered as she steadied her hand. Then Jay was writing something, too. It was all very hazy, like a dream.

They left the church, and Jay took hold of her arm.

'OK, that's it. Time we were heading back.'

Mrs Travers, he had called her, and she was still puzzling over it when they reached the small airfield.

Jay was deep in conversation with someone, and from the sound of his voice, what he was being told didn't please him.

'There's a storm brewing up,' he told her curtly. 'A real bad one. We'll have to stay here tonight. There's a hotel in town. We'll have to go back there.'

The fogginess blocking her thought processes was clearing slightly, but not enough for her to make any sense of the situation. She couldn't understand what she was doing out here in the middle of nowhere with Jay, or why she should have that worrying memory of him referring to her as 'Mrs Travers'.

Perhaps if she just kept quiet it would all fall into place properly. Perhaps none of this was actually real, and she was just having a dream.

She nipped her arm with her fingers, and grimaced ruefully as she rubbed at the resultant sore spot. She *wasn't* dreaming!

'Come on.'

Jay took hold of her arm and hustled her back to the waiting car. He said something to the driver in a language that was vaguely familiar. She had heard it somewhere recently.

Dolores... She had a momentary vision of the Mexican woman talking to her husband. That was it! The language Jay was speaking was Mexican. But what were they *doing* in Mexico?

As they drove back into town, they went into a dusty, ill-lit square, dominated at one end by the dignified simplicity of the small white church.

The church. Through her confused thoughts trailed provocative wisps of memory: a priest...incense...an altar...familiar words.

Her mind cleared, and she looked at Jay, exclaiming stupidly, 'We're married!'

He wasn't looking at her. His hands were clenched on his knees.

'Yes, and we can be divorced just as soon as you put your name to a piece of paper giving up all your rights under my grandfather's will!'

All her rights... That included her co-guardianship of the twins... She frowned as the muzziness swept back. The car stopped, and she stumbled slightly as she got out. Jay supported her, but there was no tenderness in his hold.

No tenderness... She shuddered deeply, remembering, dark shamed colour stinging her face as she recalled how willingly she had allowed him to bemuse her.

'I was drunk,' she said quietly. 'I didn't know what I was doing. The priest...'

As though he knew what she was going to say, Jay interrupted mockingly, 'I told him that you'd over indulged in a pre-wedding celebration.'

'And he believed you?' She could hardly credit it.

'You didn't need any persuasion to make the right responses,' he told her drily. 'In fact...'

She didn't want to hear any more. She was beginning to have distinctly disturbing flashes of memory. Of herself clinging to him, of being kissed by him and wanting those kisses. She groaned and touched her pounding head. What on earth had possessed her? And how much had she actually had to drink?

'I don't normally drink. I don't have any alcohol tolerance.' She was shivering now, and angry with herself for telling him this.

His eyebrows rose. 'Really?'

She hated the mockery in his voice as he drawled, 'That brandy was a special one ordered by the old man. It's strong stuff, and best left to those who can handle it.'

He was laughing at her, damn him! Natasha clenched her fists and knew impotently that there was nothing she could do. He had been remarkably quick to take advantage of her folly; but *she* was the one who had given him the opportunity to do so. *She* was the one to blame for this ridiculous farce of a marriage.

They were outside the dusty entrance to a small hotel, and Jay opened the door to it for her, ignoring her smothered gasp of dismay.

The desk clerk raised his head and surveyed them sleepily.

'We want two rooms for the night,' Jay told him.

'Two rooms? Sorry, *señor*, there is only one. The others, they are all full up.'

She heard Jay swear under his breath. 'OK. We'll take it.'

The clerk handed him an old-fashioned, heavy key, and gave him directions in Mexican.

Natasha waited until they were out of earshot of the clerk, before stating positively. 'I'm *not* sharing a room with you—marriage or no marriage...'

'Don't flatter yourself. You're in no danger from me. Like I already told you, I don't go in for other men's leavings...'

'Not even when the other man is your brother?' Natasha said cynically.

The look he gave her could have split stone, and she instantly wished her acid remark unsaid.

'In here,' Jay directed, stopping outside a door and unlocking it.

The room was small and fusty, the heat barely dispelled by an old-fashioned ceiling fan.

'Bath's over there,' Jay told her, indicating a door in the far wall. 'Use it if you want to, and then we'd both better try to get some sleep.'

For a man who had just kidnapped her and forced her into an unwanted marriage, he seemed remarkably unconcerned.

'I'm not sharing this room with you,' Natasha repeated coldly, only to suddenly feel the cotton-woolly sensation cloud her brain once again. Not as strong this time, but enough to make her forget what it was she had been about to say and instead to put a hand to her head and cling to the edge of the bed.

She heard Jay saying something to her and knew that he was angry, but she no longer cared. An inescapable tiredness was claiming her, sending her to sleep almost where she stood. She heard herself speak in a drugged, slurred voice that she barely recognised as her own, and then she was being picked up, placed down on the bed, which proved to be surprisingly comfortable. Someone spoke to her, demanding something, but she rolled over on to her front to block out the sound, letting the waves of sleep wash over her and carry her deeper and deeper into unconsciousness.

She came to slowly, conscious that all was not as it should be, but unable to identify the reason why, until she realised that she was not alone in the strange bed, and furthermore that she was not wearing a nightgown, but instead seemed to be dressed only in her bra and briefs.

She turned her head, flinching away from the sight of Jay's dark head on the pillow next to her own. She was in bed with Jay...

It took several minutes for that to sink in and, while it did, other things began to surface. Blurred memories of a night-time flight, of a church and a wedding...

She sat bolt upright, shock coursing through her. She and Jay were married! He had married her so that she couldn't marry Adam, so that he wouldn't lose half of the ranch. He had married her and, in doing so, had fulfilled his grandfather's plans for him.

But they couldn't *stay* married. She couldn't remain married to a man who despised her, who had kidnapped her... who had stated quite plainly how much he loathed and detested her... Just as she loathed and detested him! Didn't she? That other thing, that sensation that uncurled inside her every time he touched her, that was just a regrettable physical reaction—nothing important, nothing that needed to be taken into consideration.

She turned her head unwillingly and looked down at him. He was still deeply asleep. Black lashes curling against the hard jut of cheekbones shadowing the bronzed planes of his face. His jaw was dark with overnight stubble.

Why was she sitting here gazing at him like this? Why wasn't she making her escape, leaving while she could, so that she could expose him for what he had done to her? There was nothing to stop her from going. Nothing at all...

She moved tentatively towards the side of the bed, her whole body going rigid as a hand shot out and grabbed her wrist, a sleep slurred voice demanding, 'Just where do you think you're going?'

'To the bathroom. I...'

Weakly, she said the first thing that came into her head, making an ineffectual grab for the sheet when she realised how much of her body was exposed to him.

The white lace of her bra concealed very little, and she felt hot colour scorch her face as his eyes raked her body in a swiftly comprehensive glance.

'There's no need to act the shy virgin with me— I know it all, remember?' he derided softly.

Much as she longed to tell him that, on the contrary, he knew nothing, Natasha kept her lips pressed tightly together. The last thing she needed now was to get involved in another blistering argument with him.

It had gradually come to her how dependent she was on him. She was in a foreign country, a strange town. She had no money, no documents, nothing. If he chose to walk out and leave her here... She shuddered inwardly.

Of course, she could always ring Adam, but how on earth could she explain to him what had happened? How on earth could anyone believe that she had actually been drunk and married against her will? It all sounded far too preposterous.

'What are you waiting for?' Jay goaded her. 'Me to turn my back?'

His sarcasm hurt. Refusing to respond to it, she slipped out of the bed, quickly gathering up her clothes where they had been folded and left on a chair, and hurrying into the bathroom.

Jay must have undressed her last night. At least he had had the decency to leave her with the brief covering of her underwear... She was surprised that he hadn't simply let her sleep in her clothes.

She showered quickly in the rust-stained shower, wishing she had something more than a handkerchief with which to clean her teeth. But then, she had scarcely come equipped to stay the night. And neither had Jay, she remembered, recalling his anger at the storm that had delayed them.

She glanced at her watch. It was gone eight. Already they would have been missed at the ranch. Already people must be wondering where they were.

Pulling on her dress she hurried back into the bedroom, coming to an abrupt halt as she saw Jay standing at the side of the bed, lazily rubbing the dark mat of hair that covered his chest.

He smiled tauntingly when he saw her.

'What's wrong? Never seen a *real* man before? You should be more choosy about whom you sleep with.'

She wanted to hit him, throw something at him! But caution stopped her. Despite his taunting words, there was a look in his eyes that warned her of the likely physical response any attack on her part would encourage.

It gave her no pleasure to realise that physically he wanted her. She averted her eyes from his body and said in a strained voice, 'It's gone eight. They'll be wondering where we are...at the ranch.'

'Yes, we'd better get back.'

While he was in the bathroom, she toyed with the idea of leaving, but knew that it was impossible. How far could she get on foot and with no money? No, it was better to wait until they got to the ranch before she made any attempt to extricate herself from the situation.

Hadn't he said something about a divorce last night? Her forehead crinkled in a frown. Something about her signing the ranch over to him?

She almost laughed aloud, as she reflected how unnecessary his abduction of her had been. If he had only known it, she had been about to break the terms of the will herself.

'What are you going to tell them when we get back to the ranch?' Natasha demanded half an hour later when they were airborne and heading back to Texas.

'Why, that we went and got married, of course,' Jay told her lazily.

'It will be the shortest marriage on record! The first thing I'm going to do is to go into Dallas and...'

'And what? Tell your boyfriend?'

'No, find myself a lawyer who can draw up an agreement that will set me free from this farce.'

Jay said nothing, and Natasha was forced to settle back into her seat in frustrated silence.

The moment they touched down, a vehicle appeared, throwing up a cloud of dust.

Rory was driving it, curiosity written quite plainly on his face as he watched them both alight from the plane.

'Sure have caused a fuss and commotion down at the homestead,' he commented laconically as they got into the truck. 'Those two kids have been fussing and fretting over you fit to beat the band, wondering where you was gone to.'

This last comment he addressed to Natasha alone. Her heart, frozen into a state of numb shock by the events of the night, thawed a little.

'Quit talking and keep driving, Rory,' Jay demanded. 'It's been a long night.'

For some reason the drawled comment sounded full of hidden meanings and Natasha felt herself blushing. Now Rory would probably surmise that the two of them had sneaked away for a . . . for a night of uninterrupted sex, and there was nothing she could do to correct that misapprehension.

Rory stopped outside the ranch. Jay climbed out first, and then helped her down. She wrenched away from him, anger darkening her eyes, resentment for his false concern filling her.

'You're back . . . Where have you *been*?'

Cherry came racing out to greet them, Rosalie not far behind.

'Yes. We thought you must have gone to Dallas, but——' She broke off and looked over her shoulder at the man following her.

Natasha stopped dead. Adam was standing frowning at her, his mouth a tight line of resentment.

'We telephoned him, because we thought you must have gone to see him,' Cherry explained, her eyes going from Jay's unreadable face to Natasha's pale one.

'Yes, and he said you hadn't, and then he got someone to fly him right out here.'

'Natasha! What the *hell's* going on?'

Adam came up to her, his hand grasping her arm, hurting her almost.

Almost instantly Jay was standing between them, his shadow threatening that of the small man.

'Take your hands off my wife,' he said quietly. 'Or do I have to make you?'

His words had the effect of a gun going off. Everyone froze and then stared at Natasha.

The twins recovered first, racing over to her, and flinging their arms round her.

'You did it! You did it!' Cherry chanted. 'You made Uncle Jay fall in love with you. I knew you would.'

Rosalie was not as vocal, but her pleasure was as evident as her twin's.

Dolores who had appeared in the doorway, relaxed her grim stance and smiled. Of all of them, only she and Adam seemed to be unable to make any sort of response.

Adam was staring at her as though he had never seen her before, while Jay remained at her side, very much the proud and protective husband. Unless one happened to know the truth, Natasha thought bitterly.

She ached to cry out that it was all a farce, that he had only married her out of greed and spite, but somehow the words wouldn't come, and then Adam's hand fell away from her arm, and he was turning away from her.

Soon he would leave, and he wouldn't come back ... She knew that ...

'You're a fool, Natasha,' he told her as he left. 'He's only marrying you so that he can have full control of this place.'

She didn't need Adam to tell her that. Behind her, Jay made a sound of satisfaction.

'You've lost him now,' he told her mockingly. 'He thinks you've sold out to the higher bidder.'

Much as she longed to vent her misery and rage on him, Natasha controlled herself. A barrier of cold indifference behind which she could withdraw was her best defence now.

She left him and walked into the house, the twins following her, plying her with eager questions.

'Now, you just let her alone,' Dolores told them, adding scoldingly to Natasha, 'Running off and getting married in the middle of the night! Whoever heard of such a thing...'

'But it must have been really romantic,' Cherry interrupted dreamily. 'Uncle Jay must really love you, Natasha.'

What could she say? She sank down into a chair and accepted Dolores's offer of coffee, shaking her head when the housekeeper suggested that she might also want something to eat.

'You're losing weight,' the Mexican woman told her disapprovingly. 'Jay should have waited until a quieter time of the year and taken you away for a proper honeymoon... Paris. Now that would be a fine thing.'

Why on earth was everyone persisting in believing that she and Jay had married for love? Surely it must be overwhelmingly obvious that no such emotion existed between them? In the twins she could understand it—just—they desperately wanted to re-create the sense of family they had lost with their parents' death. But Dolores...

surely she could see that there was no love in Jay's eyes when he looked at her?

A terrible weariness enveloped her. There was nothing she wanted more than to go and lie down in her room, but how could she?

To one side of her the twins were prattling away happily, and to the other Dolores was saying something about organising a barbecue and party to celebrate their marriage. Jay would have to deal with that, she thought tiredly, putting her hand to her aching head.

Her mouth felt dry; a legacy from the brandy she had drunk. Her stomach heaved queasily at the memory.

She shuddered a little. She had known Jay could be ruthless—but to marry her against her will? It was a marriage that wouldn't last for very long, she reminded herself comfortingly. Just as soon as she could, she would make sure it was dissolved. Jay would let her go willingly enough once she had handed over half of the ranch to him.

Since it was a busy time with the cattle, Jay, thankfully, was away from the house. When Natasha refused any lunch with a pale-faced, lacklustre smile, Dolores took charge of the twins, banishing them with the admonition that they were to let Natasha have some peace.

'You go out and sit on the veranda,' Dolores suggested. 'You won't be bothered out there. I'll send someone out with a jug of my home-made lemonade.'

She rather liked being cosseted, Natasha discovered, giving in to Dolores' unexpected spoiling. It had been a long time since anyone had fussed over her like this... Now that she and Jay were married Dolores seemed to view her in a different light. Her original antagonism had been replaced by an almost motherly concern.

Natasha didn't deceive herself that this concern was entirely for her. She suspected it was partially, at least, her status as Jay's wife that had given rise to it.

Even so, it was pleasant to relax in one of the lounging chairs in the shade of the veranda, and simply lie back and close her eyes.

If she had been feeling more energetic she could have gone for a swim in the pool, but she simply couldn't raise the enthusiasm.

One of the girls Dolores employed to help her in the kitchen and around the house came out with a tray of lemonade. She gave Natasha a shy smile and she put it down.

The same longing to sleep which had enveloped her earlier, returned, but now she could give in to it, closing her eyes and letting her body relax.

The twins woke her, announcing that she had been asleep for hours and that it was almost time for dinner.

'Uncle Jay's back. He's in the den, making some phone calls,' Rosalie told her, as they all went inside.

Jay. She shivered slightly... Her husband! Only he wasn't, not really... Panic swept through her. Why had she slept the afternoon away? Why hadn't she been on the phone to her solicitor, trying to extricate herself from this unwanted marriage?

The lethargy that had dogged her all day still clung to her body. She shivered again... Jay was such a ruthless man, so determined to get what he wanted, so determined to see her in the worst of all possible lights.

She went upstairs to her room and opened the door into the sitting-room. The personal belongings she had left on the small writing desk had gone.

Uneasily she walked into the bedroom. It was pristinely immaculate; no trace of her possessions anywhere. Her panic increased. She opened a cupboard door... empty...

She heard a sound behind her and swung round. Jay lounged against the doorframe, his arms folded, his eyes watching her movements.

'Where are all my things?'

'Where do you think? In my room! Dolores had them moved there this afternoon.'

For a moment she was too shocked to speak. She could only stare at him, trying to absorb what he was telling her. This couldn't be happening... Dolores would never... but as far as Dolores knew they were a perfectly ordinary married couple. But they *weren't* and they never could be.

'Well, she can just move them back again.' She had got her voice back, but it sounded odd, rusty and unfamiliar. 'No way am I sharing a room with you.'

'My feelings exactly,' Jay agreed, folding his arms, and giving her a gritty look, 'but you seem to be forgetting something... The twins, and apparently everyone else around here as well, seem to think we're in love.'

Natasha looked at him, her mouth compressing, disliking the meaning cloaked within the words.

'That's not my fault,' she assured him.

'No?'

The silky disbelief in the one word sent shivers down her spine.

'No!' she reiterated firmly.

'Then how do you explain away Cherry's congratulatory comment to you this morning?' His eyebrows lifted interrogatively, and to her chagrin, Natasha felt her face flush guiltily.

'It wasn't what you think. Rosalie and Cherry...'

How could she explain to him the twins' fear that he would marry Jenneth, and their subsequent, entirely innocent, suggestion that she should try to make him fall in love with her instead?

'I must admit this isn't what I expected,' Jay told her, when she remained silent. 'It *was* my intention to keep our marriage...'

'A secret?' she submitted cynically.

He shrugged, 'Other than to the three interested parties, that is myself, you and your lover, yes... It was obvious that once he knew that you were married to me he would drop out of the scene.'

'Allowing you to put pressure on me to hand over my share of the ranch so that I could go with him, I suppose,' Natasha supplied angrily.

'Unfortunately, I hadn't expected him to be at the ranch waiting for us,' Jay continued, smoothly ignoring her outburst.

And of course he had had to announce their marriage to stop her from leaving with Adam, Natasha realised.

'I'm not going to share a bedroom with you,' she repeated stubbornly.

'What is it you're so afraid of?' She hated the cynical way he looked at her. 'Not me, surely?'

'How can you say that, after what you've done?' Natasha demanded heatedly, deliberately mis-understanding.

'Some people would think everything I've done is justified in view of what *you've* done to me!'

'Does the ranch really mean so much to you that you'd demean yourself by marrying a woman you so obviously despise?'

'Yes.' He looked at her, a faintly brooding expression in his eyes. 'Not in a personal sense... wealth and all its trappings,' he shrugged, 'they mean nothing. But this land, the people who have worked for it... fought for it... died for it. Yes, they're important to me. More important than my own personal feelings. I owe it to them to hold this place together, to pass it on to the next generation.'

'But you have no son,' Natasha reminded him.

He frowned, and looked at her almost as though he hadn't realised who he was talking to.

'The twins will marry, they will have children... A son, a daughter, it doesn't matter...'

It was odd that he hadn't reminded her that there was nothing to stop him having a child of his own. Had he really loved the twins' mother so much that he couldn't even endure the thought of another woman bearing his child? That didn't tie in with a personality ruthless enough to abduct, to do what had been done to her.

The door to her sitting-room opened and Dolores came in.

'Ah, there you are. I've moved your things into Jay's room,' she told Natasha unnecessarily. 'You've got ten minutes before I start to serve dinner.'

Now was her chance to tell the truth, to denounce him in front of Dolores and end this farce. But instead she found herself walking towards the door, shepherded there by Jay, who was walking alongside her.

'This way.' He touched her arm and her skin tingled dangerously.

His room was right at the end of the hallway. Unlike hers, it didn't have its own sitting-room, but it was enormous, furnished with heavily carved Spanish furniture and decorated in glowing Mexican fabrics.

The bed was huge. It had a heavy carved headboard, and a traditional patchwork quilt covered the bed. It looked large enough to sleep four adults with ease, and yet Natasha felt herself looking away from it, her stomach muscles knotting with tension.

Jay had been right about one thing. She had nothing to fear from him sexually. The desire she had sensed in him when he kissed her previously had been totally absent since their marriage and, besides, she had always known how much he resented feeling it.

'Bathroom's over here,' Jay told her, striding into the room and pushing open a door. 'This room used to belong to my parents, but I only moved in here after Gramps died. Dressing-room's through there.' He opened another door and Natasha walked through it into a long narrow room, the length of which ran fitted wardrobes. She opened one and saw all her dresses hanging neatly inside it. The wardrobe doors were mirror-fronted and the room itself was almost as large as the small bedroom of her London flat.

If ony there was a chair in it she could have slept in here instead of sharing Jay's bed.

'I need to take a shower,' she heard Jay saying behind her. 'We'd better get a move on, otherwise Dolores will be lambasting us for being late for dinner.'

How long would it take him to shower? Natasha wondered feverishly, closing the dressing-room door behind her and quickly tugging off her jeans and top. *She* would have liked a shower too, but she wasn't going to risk running into Jay in a state of undress.

The moment she was changed she went downstairs. The twins looked surprised to see her without Jay.

Why on earth hadn't she told them right from the start that they were living in a dream world in imagining that she and Jay were going to live happily ever after?

The answer to that was simple enough—she hadn't wanted to disappoint them with the truth, and now she was going to have to pay for that weakness.

CHAPTER NINE

ALL through dinner Natasha was on edge, surreptitiously watching Jay, while trying to appear lighthearted and happy for the twins.

When he announced that he had some work to do, she gave a tiny, unconscious sigh of relief, silencing the girls' protests.

With any luck, his work would keep him in his study until she was safely upstairs and asleep.

She saw the twins off to bed, and made a pretence of reading a magazine, anxiously waiting as the minutes ticked by until she could reasonably go upstairs, praying that Jay wouldn't emerge from his den until she had done so.

She had no illusions left. If he were to guess how she felt about sharing a room with him, he would take a fiendish delight in enforcing an unwanted intimacy on her. She shuddered tensely, a fine film of sweat breaking out on her skin.

It was gone ten o'clock at last. She put down the magazine and walked shakily upstairs.

In the unfamiliar bedroom, she found her nightclothes and headed for the bathroom.

The enormous half-sunken bath tempted her, but she dared not linger. Who had had it installed? It was easily large enough to accommodate two... Her mouth went dry, her pulses racing as she closed her mind against the unwanted mental image of Jay sharing the bathroom's sensual intimacy with someone... Had he ever brought the twins' mother here? Had she...

No, she must *not* think like that...

She showered, quickly rubbing herself until her skin glowed, before donning her cotton nightdress.

On the threshold of the bedroom she hesitated, glancing unhappily at the bed. Large though it was, she didn't want to share it with Jay. She didn't want... She didn't want anything to do with him, she told herself firmly, ignoring the tiny frisson of sexual awareness that spread through her body. How could it be that she could feel this sexual hunger for a man whom logic told her she should hate and despise?

She looked frantically around the room, desperately searching for a means of escape. Her glance clung to the door to the dressing-room. She could sleep in there on a chair... It would be uncomfortable, but better than sharing Jay's bed...

The only chair that was suitable was a heavy armchair that she only just managed to drag into the narrow space. Her arms ached from the effort of moving it; her heart was thudding with fearful dread in case Jay should walk in and discover what she was doing.

She had no idea where she might find some spare bedding, so she snatched a pillow from the bed, and a huge, fluffy bath towel from the carefully folded pile in the bathroom, and then, wrapping this round her, curled up as best she could in the armchair.

She wasn't very comfortable, and each time she tried to find a way of easing a new ache, she thought longingly of the huge bed, but then the memory of

Jay stopped her from going to it. He might have forced her into this marriage, and into a mould that was completely false to her real nature, but there were some things he could not force her to do.

She would show him that she had grit and determination to match his; that she couldn't be pushed around, bullied, despised and condemned...

Drowsily, her muddled thoughts tailed off as exhaustion eased her cramped limbs into sleep.

She didn't hear the door to the bedroom open just under an hour later, nor see the quick tension that gripped Jay's body as he saw the empty bed, but she did feel the warm strength in the arms that plucked her from her cramped impromptu bed, and some instinct buried deep inside her surfaced through her sleep, making her snuggle seekingly against him.

Her body registered the coolness of his withdrawal when he put her down, and she turned instinctively towards him, her forehead puckered in a faint frown, her cramped limbs relaxing into the spaciousness of the bed.

Jay studied her frowningly for several seconds before straightening up. What was it about this woman that sparked off such a fierce burn of desire within him? He knew what she was, and he had wanted women before. But never quite like this, he admitted broodingly, ruthlessly subduing the ache building up inside him; never quite like this.

Despite the comfort of the large bed, Natasha's sleep was restless. She moved unceasingly, turning over and reaching out as though in search of something.

She turned over and came to rest against something warm and solid. Her body relaxed on a small sigh as it ceased its restless questing, her sleep deepening as she snuggled closer to Jay's sleeping frame.

It was a nightmare that woke her, a sickening, frightening sensation of being relentlessly pursued by some nameless, formless enemy that brought her out of the depths of her slumbers with a sharp cry and an abrupt movement that woke Jay as well.

It took her several seconds to realise she wasn't alone in bed, and then several more to remember that she ought to have been sleeping in the armchair.

'What's wrong?'

The shock of hearing Jay's voice panicked her, sending her instinctively towards the far edge of the bed. His fingers manacled her wrist before she got there, keeping her imprisoned.

'Let me go,' Natasha demanded. 'If you think I'm sharing this bed with you . . .'

The smile that curled his mouth silenced her, making a shiver of fear tremor through her muscles. It was a cruel, cynical smile, edged with bitterness.

'Is that a fact? Then just how do you account for the fact that less than an hour ago you couldn't wait to get just as close to me as you possibly could?'

'That's a lie . . . I was sleeping in the dressing-room.'

'Yes, where anyone, including the twins, could have walked in and seen you,' Jay agreed angrily. 'I'm not talking about that,' his voice was scornful. 'I'm talking about the way, the moment you got in this bed, you clung to me like ivy hugs a wall.'

'No!' The husky denial ripped from her throat in an agonised sound of distress.

She felt Jay reach towards her with his free hand and she flinched away in the semi-darkness, but he was only switching on one of the lamps.

'Yes,' he told her gratingly, capturing her chin and turning her face so that she had to look at him.

He wasn't wearing a pyjama top, and his skin glowed like polished gold in the lamplight. His chest rose and fell sharply as he breathed, anger glittering in his eyes. Like a woodland creature fascinated by the gaze of a hunter, Natasha felt her gaze cling helplessly to the hard outline of his mouth.

'You're lying.' Her voice trembled. 'I wouldn't come near you for... for ten times as much as Tip left me.'

It was the wrong thing to say. She felt it in the sudden explosive compacting of his muscles.

'Well now, is that a fact?' He looked past her at the night-stand which held a collection of change and dollar bills, and said, with soft menace that brought a shudder of horror to her skin, 'I've got a hundred dollars here that says I could make you cry out for me, and want me so much that you'd be begging me to take you.'

'No!' It was the only protest she could get through her locked throat muscles—her whole body felt literally frozen with dread.

'No, what? No, I couldn't do it or...'

What was happening to her? It was like an unending nightmare that piled horror upon horror with no release!

'I'm going to turn that into a yes,' she heard Jay saying savagely. 'I'm going to show that greedy little mind of yours just exactly what it's sold out... Have you ever given yourself to any man just for the pleasure of it, Natasha?' he asked her softly.

He was stroking the inner skin of her wrist hypnotically, with fingers that made her flesh tingle and her body quiver. She was desperately afraid of the purpose she read in his eyes, but she knew that there was no way he was going to let her go.

'Before tonight's over, I'm going to make you ache and burn...' He moved, drawing her against the warm hardness of his torso, his head bending so that his mouth could explore the smooth softness of her throat, smothering words that had almost sounded like, 'The way you've done to me.'

But he could hardly have said that, she admitted feverishly, her brain clouded by her fear of the pleasure he was making her feel. Just the touch of his mouth against her skin ignited such sensations inside her! She opened her mouth to tell him to stop, but all that emerged was a soft moan. As though it had been a command in a private language, his mouth moved, probing the neckline of her nightdress, his hand tracing the shape of her spine, arching her against him.

The ribbon ties at the neckline of her nightdress gave way beneath his hands, laying her breasts bare to his gaze.

Natasha closed her eyes, caught between shame and another less easily understood sensation that made her shiver and brought her coral-pink nipples burgeoning into taut fullness.

She felt Jay slide her nightdress off her shoulders, and then his hands were cupping her breasts. She kept her eyes tightly closed.

'Yes,' she heard him say thickly. 'I always knew you would feel like this. Soft, silky.' His thumbs rubbed slowly against the hard points of her breasts, making her shudder fiercely at the surge of pleasure that rushed through her.

'So responsive, especially to a man you don't want. But then you've never wanted *any* man, have you, Natasha? You only want their money.'

She cried out wildly, pushing away from him, but he was too strong for her, his arms locking round her body so that her breasts were pressed against the hardness of his chest. She tried to breathe, and found she could only take in shallow sips of air. She struggled and gasped beneath the onslaught of strange pleasure that invaded her, as her frantic movements inadvertently dragged the hard points of her breasts against the rough darkness of Jay's body hair.

She felt the answering tension shock through Jay, and heard the sound he made deep in his chest. Then he was cupping her breasts, pressing them into his body, moving against her in a way that made her powerless to resist the flood of sensation spilling through her.

She made a sound, something between a cry and a sob, but when his hands slid down her ribcage and arched her back, so that he could bend his head and take first one and then the other swollen nipple into his mouth, she made no physical or verbal protest.

The lamplight highlighted them, etching the primitive intimacy of their embrace, her hair spilling over his arm, his body dark and golden against the silky paleness of hers, her breasts crowned by the dusky aroused buds of flesh so recently possessed by his mouth.

Way, way beyond any form of rational thought, Natasha could only cling to the hardness of his arms, her mind and her body completely overwhelmed by the sensations induced by the spearing intimacy of his mouth. She shuddered deeply, torn by the enormity of what he had made her feel, her eyes tightly closed, her lashes black smudges against the paleness of her skin, her mouth a vulnerable curve of pink.

She didn't see Jay frown as he felt her tremble and looked into her shadowed face. Her reaction had caught him off guard. It hadn't been what he had expected at all... He could almost have believed that no man had ever... She was an even better actress than he had supposed, he decided bitterly, releasing her so abruptly that she fell across the bed.

Natasha opened her eyes, shock and pain coursing through her. 'Well,' she heard Jay demand harshly, 'do you still claim that you don't want to share my bed? That you...'

She covered her ears so that she couldn't hear any more. Tears clogged her throat... She felt as though she had been abused in the most painful way there was—not physically but emotionally. She wanted to crawl away somewhere and die. She wanted... she wanted to be back in Jay's arms, his hands and mouth caressing her skin. She wanted... she wanted him in the most intense and shockingly intimate way there was, she acknowledged achingly. She wanted him to make love to her, real love... not this—this parody of desire...

Mercifully he let her crawl away to the other side of the bed, and as he switched off the lamp her body relaxed on a tormented breath of relief. He wasn't going to touch her again. She knew she couldn't have resisted him if he had. Her skin burned with shame, her body tormented by physical longing she knew would never be satisfied.

'Didn't manage to hold out for very long, did you?' Jay tormented her savagely. 'God, I could have...'

He stopped abruptly and then said cruelly, 'I think I begin to understand the hold you have on your victims. That's one hell of a mighty fine act you've got yourself there, lady.'

She couldn't let that pass. She had been struggling to do up the ties on her nightdress, but now she stopped, wincing as the fine cotton brushed against the still aroused outline of her breasts.

'I don't...'

'What? Give all your lovers the pleasure of the performance you've just given me? You should do. I know men who'd part with millions for a reaction like that, and after all, we're all the same to a woman like you, aren't we? Who do you think about when you close your eyes? Your first lover? Your bank account?'

Through the darkness, the tension that gripped her body reached him. A sense of desolation washed over him, and he lay down with his back to her. He couldn't blame Tip for doing what he'd done, not any more. God, he himself... He blanked off the thought deliberately, willing himself to put the woman lying in bed beside him, and everything to do with her, out of his mind.

Long after Jay's deep, even breathing signalled
the fact that he was asleep, Natasha lay awake. The
tears which had slid silently from her eyes under
the onslaught of his insults had dried, leaving her
skin feeling tight and sore.

She couldn't stay here now. Somehow she would
have to find a way to leave. She ought never to have
allowed him to force her into this marriage. She
hadn't tried anything like hard enough to dissuade
him... Because secretly, she hadn't wanted to dissuade him, she realised. She hadn't wanted to dissuade him because... because she loved him.

'No!' She mouthed the word, her throat dry, her
eyes stinging as she fought against what her heart
was telling her. How *could* she love him? How could
any woman love a man who treated her the way
Jay had treated her? Who believed that she was
nothing more than...

She tried to push the thought away, to deny it,
or to explain away her feelings by some means of
logic and analysis, but it was no use.

Here in the short, dark hours of the night, the
truth refused to be banished. She was in love with
Jay. How? Why? When? All these were questions
she could not answer. She only knew that when he
looked at her, spoke to her, touched her, something
happened to her that had never happened before.

No, she couldn't stay here now, her pride dis-
integrating, her heart and body aching for him, her
will-power slowly destroyed by the need eating into
her as she waited for the day when his anger, or
his physical hunger, brought him to her. If they
made love, he would know the truth, but that would
not alter his lack of feelings for her. Knowing that

she was innocent of the charges he had brought against her would not change his feelings for her.

He had married her because of Tip's will. Very well then, she would do what she had planned to do originally. She would go home to England and get her solicitor to draft out a document by which she could rescind her interest in the ranch. She would leave. She *had* to leave. But how?

When Natasha woke up, it was in the knowledge that something unbearable and earth-shattering had taken place. It was several seconds before she remembered what. She was so used to denying her feelings, to hiding from them, that at first she could almost pretend that it had all been a mistake, that she didn't love Jay at all. But she only had to remember what had happened last night, to feel again the same mixture of pain and need that had brought the truth to her the night before. She loved him, and perhaps, deep down inside, she had let him marry her, hoping that by some miracle he might come to love her too.

She was too old for such foolish hopes. They were best left to the twins.

She was alone in the bedroom, and that seemed to underline the impossibility of her folly. She got up listlessly, dressing in the first thing that came to hand.

Dolores gave her a shrewd and concerned glance as she walked into the breakfast-room, but she was too caught up in her own thoughts to see it.

The twins greeted her eagerly. 'You're late. Uncle Jay's down with the cattle... Are you going down to see him?'

Natasha shook her head.

'When I went out to feed Nobby this morning, Jake was polishing your car. Are you ever going to drive it?'

Her *car*! Of course, she had forgotten all about the Mercedes... She could drive it to Dallas, leave it there and board a plane for home.

Nearly until dawn she had lain awake wondering how she could get away without alerting anyone to what she was doing, and she had never once thought about the car.

'Of course. In fact, I think I might give it a trial run today.' She tried to sound nonchalant, keeping her eyes fixed on her coffee-cup as she spoke.

'Great! Can we come with you?'

'Not this time. I'd like to get the feel of her before I take any passengers.'

It appalled her how easily the lies came to her lips. It just showed what the human psyche was capable of when the need arose.

Please God the twins wouldn't hate her when they realised that she had gone... One day, when they were adult, perhaps she would be able to explain to them just why she had had to go. If only Jay was more approachable, less inclined to believe the absolute worst of her, she might have been able to talk to him, to persuade him to let her go.

But if that had been the case she wouldn't have been in the situation she was, she reminded herself miserably.

Dolores offered her more coffee. She raised her head and saw that the Mexican woman was frowning slightly.

'You all right?' she asked as Natasha refused.

'A little tired, that's all.' Her skin flushed brightly as she said the words, and she bit down hard into her bottom lip, hoping that Dolores would put her behaviour down to bridal shyness. She hated having to lie like this, to plot and plan, but she had to get away. If she didn't, she would be reduced to little more than a sexual toy that Jay could take up or put down as he pleased, and she had too much pride for that. She would kill herself rather than be reduced to that fate, she told herself fiercely.

It was an impossible situation. She loved Jay too much to withstand him if he did start to make love to her, and once he knew the truth he would probably still despise her for not being strong enough to resist him.

Manlike, he would take all that she had to offer and give nothing in return, other than the physical intimacy of his body. And that was something she didn't think she could endure.

She made her plans carefully, packing her cases while the twins were out riding, waiting until she knew Dolores would be busy in the kitchen before taking them down to the car.

Luckily the garage area was deserted, but her body was shaking after she had finished stacking them into the boot. She locked it and returned to the house. She had already decided that she would wait to leave until just after lunch. That way no one would be suspicious about her absence until she missed dinner.

By then she would be safely in Dallas, and perhaps even on board a plane for home.

Home. Why did it have such a mournful sound? Why did she feel so wretchedly miserable about the thought of leaving? Because she was leaving the man she loved ... That was why.

CHAPTER TEN

ALL round her the flat landscape shimmered under the appalling heat of the mid-afternoon sun. Even with the car's air-conditioning working on full, Natasha could still feel perspiration soaking her body.

Of course, it wasn't all entirely heat induced. There was an element of fear and apprehension in the fierce burning of her skin and the rapid thump of her heart, Natasha acknowledged, wiping her sticky hand on her skirt before returning it to the wheel.

She had no idea how far she was from Dallas. She had been driving for over two hours, and there was absolutely nothing at all in sight, but at least she had managed to get away without being spotted.

The ranch had its own petrol supply and she had filled up the car's tank before she left. It was over three hundred miles to Dallas, but she should have enough, surely?

Soon she would be off Jay's land. The boundary fence must be somewhere up ahead of her. She pressed her foot down harder on the accelerator, anxious to get past that psychological barrier.

The rabbit appeared from nowhere and she braked instinctively, gasping as the impetus of her too-sudden action threw the heavy car off the tarmac. Her head hit the soft top of the car as it bounced on to the rough terrain, the steering wheel slipping from her hands.

Natasha cried out as the front wheel hit a huge boulder. The car lifted with a grating sound of expansive metal, the engine dying as the car slipped back, tilting at an uncomfortable angle.

Unfastening her seat-belt, Natasha managed to scramble out. She hurried to the front of the car, and came to an abrupt and appalled stop. The front end of the car was firmly and quite inextricably wedged on to the narrow end of the boulder. There was just no way she was going to be able to get it off.

Her first thought was that she was trapped, that she would never escape from Jay. And then, as that initial panic subsided, another and darker possibility struck her, namely that she could die out here in this burning landscape without ever being found.

It would be several hours yet before she was missed... Hours during which she would be exposed to the sun's heat on her sensitive skin. She had no water, no food. She licked her already dry lips, appalled by her own folly. Perhaps she should try and walk. But where to? Back to the ranch? It was over fifty miles! She would never do it!

No, she would just have to stay here, and hope that someone would find her.

She crawled back inside the car, and curled up on the passenger seat.

An hour crawled past. The heat inside the car was stifling, but it was just as hot outside, and outside there was no protection for her head. No, she was better off inside, she decided listlessly.

A muzzy feeling filled her head. She wanted to close her eyes and go to sleep, but something warned her that she must not. She thought she heard the sound of a car, but when she looked there was nothing... Nothing but the vastness of the Texan landscape and its empty blue sky.

She dozed, drained of energy by the heat. She woke suddenly, her lips framing a name her throat was too dry to speak.

'Jay.'

'Just what in hell do you think you're playing at?'

She blinked and blinked again, not convinced that he wasn't a mirage. A truck was parked alongside her car, but she hadn't even heard it draw up. Jay was taking hold of her, almost dragging her out of the stifling car.

'You little fool!' he shook her roughly. 'Don't you know you could have died out here?'

'Then why didn't you let me?'

The waspish words were out before she could stop them, followed by tears that filmed her eyes and made her shake horribly.

She turned away as Jay put her down, half stumbling because of the numbness in her cramped limbs. She heard Jay swear and then she was back in his arms, being carried over to the cab of the truck.

He closed the door on her and returned to her car, opening the boot and removing her cases.

It was only when he started the truck's engine that she realised they were leaving.

'My car,' she protested.

'I'll send someone out to salvage it. Have you no sense in your head?' he demanded thickly. 'God, didn't your common sense tell you that...'

He broke off as she shuddered. They were sitting so close together that her body was pressed against his, and there was no way she could stop him from feeling the reaction coursing through her.

'I...I'm thirsty.'

He swore again, stopping the truck, and reaching behind him for a flask which he handed to her.

'Drink it slowly,' he advised her. 'You haven't been out for long enough to have suffered real dehydration, but even so, if you drink too fast you could get sick...'

He had put the truck back on the road, but instead of heading back for the ranch he was driving in the opposite direction.

'Where are you taking me?'

He gave her a derisive look.

'Not where you want to go... You and I have got some talking to do before I let you go anywhere.'

'We don't have anything to talk about,' Natasha protested miserably. 'I'm going to rescind my interest in Tip's will. I...I have to get away from here.'

The admission was made before she could stop it, and she couldn't bear to look at Jay when he brought the truck to a screeching halt.

She waited for him to make some blistering sardonic comment, but when he spoke he said shatteringly, 'Have you any idea what it did to me when Dolores told me that you'd gone?'

Stupidly all she could say was, 'I didn't think you'd find out until after dinner...'

'If it hadn't been for Dolores I shouldn't have done, but she was...concerned about you...' He frowned and stared out of the truck window. An odd sort of tension filled the enclosed space.

'Natasha——'

'Jay——'

They both spoke together and then fell silent, and then astonishingly Jay said curtly, in an oddly constrained voice, 'I don't care how many other men there've been, from now on there's only going to be me. I can't let you go, Natasha. Stay with me... I love you.' He said it simply, looking directly at her. 'And it's slowly sending me out of my mind. I've tried to tell myself that I'm a fool, that a man should run a mile before he lets himself get involved with... It doesn't matter... None of it matters...when it comes down to it. Stay with me. We could make a fresh start, forget about the past.'

A painful, disbelieving joy filled her. Jay *loved* her. She looked at him, searching his face for the signs that would tell her that he was lying; that it was all some sort of elaborate trap, but there were none. All she could see were lines of strain and dread etched into his skin, a pain in his eyes that mirrored her own.

'Jay, there's something I must tell you,' she began softly, but he stopped her.

'No! No explanations...no confessions.' His hands gripped hers, so tightly she thought her bones might crack. 'Just you and me and a clean start. Say it, Natasha... Say you'll stay with me.'

There were so many things she wanted to say, so many explanations, so many truths he didn't yet know, but it seemed he wanted to hear only one thing and so she sighed softly, 'I'll stay.'

She didn't know what she had expected his reaction to be, but it was a shock when he simply restarted the truck without a word.

'We're going the wrong way,' she pointed out timidly after a few minutes.

'No, we're not,' Jay corrected her, but he didn't say anything else, and when after several miles he turned off the road and down along a narrow dust track, he explained tersely, 'There's a shack down here where I used to camp out as a boy. The men still use it at times when they're checking the fences. We'll be there soon.'

But he hadn't told her why he was taking her there, Natasha thought, as he settled back into silence.

The shack was slightly larger than she had visualised, and the first thing that struck her when Jay stopped the truck was the emptiness of their surroundings. He got out of the truck and helped her down. She could feel the fierce thud of his heart against her body as he held her.

It reminded her of something—something she had to say to him.

'Jay, you say you love me, but Jenneth told me that...that you loved the twins' mother...that you and she were going to run away together.'

'It's not true. Helen told Jenneth that to break us up,' he frowned darkly. 'My grandfather never wanted Nat and Helen to marry. He tried his best to stop them. Helen was a gold-digger, Gramps said, and he was right. Helen never loved anyone but herself. She tried to cause trouble between Nat and me, purely out of malice. She was always threatening to leave. When she did, he went after her and they were both killed.'

'And Jenneth?'

'Jenneth was the girl next door. There was a time when I thought we'd marry but, like Helen, she was more interested in the Travers name and money than the man who went with it.'

There was a small silence, and so much that she hadn't seen before was clear to Natasha now. No wonder Jay had been so ready to believe the worst of her... to believe that she was cast in the same mould as Helen and Jenneth.

Her heart went out to him, but there was something she had to say, 'But I... slept with your grandfather, and yet you say you love me?'

He shook his head, his frown deepening, his voice harsh, 'God, do you think I haven't tormented myself with that over and over again? After Nat was killed, I told myself I'd only marry if I could find a woman who was marrying me for myself; that I'd never let myself be put in the position that he was put in, running after a woman who didn't give a single damn about him, humiliated and finally killed for loving a woman who couldn't care less. But right from the start there was something about you—I don't know what, call it what you will—that made it impossible for me to shut you out no matter how much I tried.

'I'm not going to say it's going to be easy. There'll be times when I'll hurt like hell because of your past, and when I'll probably put you through hell for it too, but I can't stop thinking about last night...about how you felt in my arms...about the way you responded to me...I *can't* believe all that was faked, Natasha,' he finished huskily. 'I *can't* believe that the way you responded to me was anything but real.'

'But last night you said——'

'Forget what I said last night,' he demanded huskily, groaning suddenly as he caught her up in his arms. 'I don't know what you've done to me, woman. I think you must have bewitched me... Right here and now I don't give a damn how many other men there have been.'

But he *did* care, Natasha realised, caught up on a wave of love and compassion, no longer doubting his love for her, wanting only to reach out to him and wipe out all the misunderstandings that had dogged their relationship.

'And...and if there haven't been any at all...will you still love me? Will you still want me, Jay?'

He was looking at her broodingly.

'Tip lied to you, Jay,' she told him softly. 'I don't know why... I know he liked to exaggerate a little. He and I were nothing more than friends—that's all. There haven't been any men in my life at all, Jay.' She gave a shaky laugh and took a step toward him. 'In fact, I'm afraid you're going to find me appallingly inexperienced. I...I hope you won't mind. I...'

She heard him give a shuddering sigh, and then she was in his arms as he carried her into the cabin, kicking the door closed behind him.

A bed with a patchwork quilt filled one wall, and he put her down on it, quickly stripping off his clothes, his eyes on her face the whole time, a smile curling his mouth when he registered her soft flush.

'It's all right. You'll soon get used to me.'

She was glad that he hadn't questioned her; that he had simply accepted her statement at face value. Explanations could come later.

She shivered slightly as the bed dipped under his weight. He didn't linger over removing her clothes, and at first she felt embarrassed at being with him like this, with full daylight pouring in through the cabin's windows and playing on their bodies, emphasising all their contrasts. But when his hands started to move over her, caressing her, she forgot her embarrassment in the wave of pleasure that engulfed her.

She clung to him unashamedly, delighting in the maleness of him against her body. Her breasts swelled into his hands, her nipples tight and eager for the moist heat of his mouth. He sucked them gently, lingering over the delicate caress until she was mindless with pleasure, opening to the touch of his hand between her thighs as though it was a ritual they had perfected over a lifetime of intimacies.

'Love me, Natasha... Love me.'

He groaned the words against her lips, kissing her with a fierce passion that made her body surge achingly against the heat of his hand.

She wanted him. She wanted him so much that it hurt. She told him as much, barely aware of what she was saying or doing as she moved frantically against him, responding to an age-old instinct that burned through her tormented flesh.

He moved, positioning himself between her thighs, his mouth hot against her skin as his body surged against hers.

Fear quickened momentarily inside her, dying beneath the swift upsurge of pleasure her body felt in its physical contact with his.

She felt him inside her and her body shook with joy. He moved powerfully and strongly, and her senses quickened.

The sudden sharp spear of pain that caught her just when she abandoned the last of her original fear made her cry out and tense, but Jay soothed her, smoothing her hair back off her hot face, kissing the soft skin of her throat and shoulder, letting her body accustom itself to him before covering her mouth with his and kissing her so deeply and intensely that her body eagerly met the rhythmic force of his, as its movements matched the deliberate penetration of her mouth by the honeyed thrust of his tongue.

Sensation after sensation arched through her, a pulsing need driving her on until she shook with the force of it, and Jay lost his grimly held control, taking her down with him into the fierce maelstrom of delight.

When the tiny ripples of pleasure started to explode through her body, she cried out in surprised delight, her eyes opening, her breath catching on a gasp as she saw the look of fierce pleasure in Jay's.

'You're mine,' he told her fiercely. 'Mine! Mine, Natasha.'

His control splintered, his body cresting the final pinnacle of pleasure and taking hers with it. She felt his lips moving gently against her skin as she fell into an exhausted sleep.

When she woke up it was dark. She was lying beneath the quilt, and at first she couldn't remember where she was. When she did, she looked anxiously for Jay.

He was crouching in front of the hearth in which he had just lit a fire. As though aware without speaking that she was awake, he looked over to her, a sombre look darkening his eyes.

He got up and came over to her, taking her hand in his.

'Can you ever forgive me?'

Tears filled her eyes.

Many, many times she had wished to see this humility, but now that she was, she hated it . . .

'I could have told you the truth, made you listen . . .'

'If there is a God up there he must surely have been guiding my steps,' Jay said sombrely. 'I acted for all the wrong reasons. Marrying you out of anger and bitterness, hating and resenting you, and yet if I hadn't married you . . . if I'd simply let you go . . . What on earth made Gramps do it?' he demanded savagely. 'Why, *why* did he leave you half the ranch? Why did he make that will? Was it because he didn't trust me? Did he ever say anything to you about it?'

Natasha shook her head.

'Nothing other than that he wanted you to marry and produce sons.' She had her own thoughts on Tip's will, but she plucked at the quilt before voicing them. 'I don't know your grandfather as well as you did, Jay, but he always struck me as a shrewd, purposeful man. Not a man who could ever be guided by sentimentality. I . . . I think he did it deliberately . . . a sort of matchmaking. You know, leaving me half the ranch, knowing that I'd have to come out here to see it. That stipulation about the twins and about staying for six months. He knew how desperately I wanted a family . . . I think he was throwing us together deliberately, and hoping that propinquity would do the rest. He'd probably forgotten all about pretending that he and I were lovers, because he knew it wasn't true.'

Jay grimaced.

'It's a lovely thought, but without wanting to hurt your feelings, my darling, Gramps wanted me to marry right enough, and he was more than capable of pulling a trick like this to achieve it. But he had it in his mind that he wanted me to marry money . . .' Jay made a gesture of disgust. 'Someone with a similar background—he never forgot what had happened to Nat.' He frowned as Natasha started laughing.

'What is it?'

It took her several minutes to calm down long enough to explain to him about her own background and the money that had come to her on the sale of the farm.

Jay was so quiet that for a few minutes she feared that she had said something wrong, that she had made a mistake after all, and that he didn't love her.

'I could kill Gramps for this,' he said quietly at last. 'When I think what I've put you through . . .'

'I could have told you the truth, proved it even. I suppose I wanted you to see it for yourself...'

'And I suspect I probably did. You appeared to be the absolute antithesis of everything I wanted in a woman, and yet I still went ahead and fell in love with you... I told myself it was just sex, but every time you looked at me you made me ache.'

'And *that's* not just sex?' Natasha teased.

'Lady,' Jay told her forcefully, 'the way it is with you and me could never be described as "just sex". However, it's plain to me that there just ain't no way you're going to believe me telling you that, so I reckon I'm just going to have to show you...'

She laughed at his exaggerated cattleman's drawl, but her laughter stopped abruptly as he took her in his arms and kissed her with a raw hunger that shocked and excited her.

He moved so that his body leaned into hers, making her aware of the arousal quickening his body.

'I hope you realise that I'm doing this for Gramps,' Jay told her when he could bring himself to release her mouth long enough to speak to her.

While he spoke, his thumb touched the swollen fullness of her lips, and she felt the fierce slam of his heart against his ribs as he saw her physical reaction to his touch.

'Gramps?' she managed to articulate tormentedly. What on earth had what he was doing to her to do with his grandfather?

'That great-grandson he wanted,' Jay murmured, his mouth just a whisper from hers. 'Something tells me that it's not going to be long before we provide him with one.'

* * *

It wasn't! Twelve months after they were married, Jay and Natasha stood side by side, watching as Rosalie and Cherry each proudly held a christening-robe-wrapped infant.

'You never told me twins ran in your family,' Jay commented to her, as Natasha kept a motherly eye on her new sons.

The fear she had once felt, the dread of revealing her feelings to him was long gone. With a grin she turned to look at him, and reminded him dulcetly, 'As I remember it, you never gave me time.'

'What are you two laughing at?' Cherry demanded curiously, experimentally juggling her white-wrapped bundle on her arm. 'Oh, I don't suppose you'll tell us. Grown-ups,' she sighed with pre-teenage acceptance of adults' strange ways, and went back to her contemplation of her new cousin.

When she and Rosalie had said they would like Natasha to marry their uncle and have a baby, they had only meant one! But still, the twins weren't too bad, and it was nice to be part of a proper family again.

'Rosalie, you are not to hold him like that!' she scolded her ten-minutes-younger sister virtuously. 'Look, you have to hold him like this!'

'How about a little holiday, once we've got these two christened?' Jay suggested, watching them.

They hadn't had a break since their marriage, and Natasha looked at him expectantly. 'Could you really get away? But where would we go?'

'Somewhere where the weather doesn't matter... You've shared my home, Natasha, but I don't know anything about yours. I thought we'd take a trip to England. Call it a delayed wedding present if you...'

He broke off to gather his wife into his arms, shaking her gently as he saw the tears in her eyes.

She still looked a little frail from the twins' birth, and his heart turned over with love for her. She meant the world to him, his quiet, beautiful wife, and he didn't think he would ever forget how nearly he had lost her.

'Well, what do you say?' he asked, masking his emotions with a smile.

'I say that I don't care where we go, as long as I'm with you.'

'Umm... Well in that case, I know this real nice secluded shack...'

They both laughed.

'No, thanks. I don't want another pair of those quite yet, thanks. I'm sure it had something to do with the water...'

'Uh huh, that's what caused it, is it?'

'Oh, come on, Rosalie,' Cherry told her sister, grimacing. 'They're going to get all soppy again.'

ATTRACTIVE, SPACE SAVING BOOK RACK

Display your most prized novels on this handsome and sturdy book rack. The hand-rubbed walnut finish will blend into your library decor with quiet elegance, providing a practical organizer for your favorite hard-or soft-covered books.

Only $9.95

Approximately 16" x 8" when assembled

Assembles in seconds!

To order, rush your name, address and zip code, along with a check or money order for $10.70* ($9.95 plus 75¢ postage and handling) payable to *Harlequin Reader Service*:

Harlequin Reader Service
Book Rack Offer
901 Fuhrmann Blvd.
P.O. Box 1396
Buffalo, NY 14269-1396

Offer not available in Canada.

*New York and Iowa residents add appropriate sales tax.

BKR-1A

*Exciting, adventurous, sensual stories
of love long ago*

On Sale Now:

SATAN'S ANGEL by Kristin James

*Slater was the law in a land that was as wild and untamed
as he was himself, but all that changed when he met
Victoria Stafford. She had been raised to be a lady, but
that didn't mean she had no will of her own. Their search
for her kidnapped cousin brought them together, but they
were too much alike for the course of true love to run
smooth.*

PRIVATE TREATY by Kathleen Eagle

*When Jacob Black Hawk rescued schoolteacher
Carolina Hammond from a furious thunderstorm, he
swept her off her feet in every sense of the word, and she
knew that he was the only man who would ever make her
feel that way. But society had put barriers between them
that only the most powerful and overwhelming love could
overcome . . .*

Look for them wherever Harlequin books are sold.   HIS-CNM-1

Temptation™

TEMPTATION WILL BE EVEN HARDER TO RESIST...

In September, Temptation is presenting a sophisticated new face to the world. A fresh look that truly brings Harlequin's most intimate romances into focus.

What's more, all-time favorite authors Barbara Delinsky, Rita Clay Estrada, Jayne Ann Krentz and Vicki Lewis Thompson will join forces to help us celebrate. The result? A very special quartet of Temptations...

- **Four striking covers**
- **Four stellar authors**
- **Four sensual love stories**
- **Four variations on one spellbinding theme**

All in one great month! Give in to Temptation in September.

TDESIGN-1